LEGION of the DEAD

Also available by Paul Stewart & Chris Riddell:

CURSE OF THE NIGHT WOLF
RETURN OF THE EMERALD SKULL

FERGUS CRANE
Winner of the Smarties Prize Gold Medal
CORBY FLOOD
Winner of the Nestlé Prize Silver Medal
HUGO PEPPER
Winner of the Nestlé Prize Silver Medal

The Quint Trilogy
THE CURSE OF THE GLOAMGLOZER
THE WINTER KNIGHTS
CLASH OF THE SKY GALLEONS

The Twig Trilogy
BEYOND THE DEEPWOODS
STORMCHASER
MIDNIGHT OVER SANCTAPHRAX

The Rook Trilogy
THE LAST OF THE SKY PIRATES
VOX
FREEGLADER

THE LOST BARKSCROLLS
THE EDGE CHRONICLES MAPS

Also available:

BLOBHEADS
BLOBHEADS GO BOING!
MUDDLE EARTH

www.stewartandriddell.co.uk

PAUL STEWART & CHRIS RIDDELL

Barnaby Grimes

LEGION of the DEAD

Illustrated by Chris Riddell

David Fickling Books

OXFORD · NEW YORK

A DAVID FICKLING BOOK

This is a work of fiction. Names, characters, places, and incidents either
are the product of the author's imagination or are used fictitiously.
Any resemblance to actual persons, living or dead, events,
or locales is entirely coincidental.

Copyright © 2008 by Paul Stewart and Chris Riddell

All rights reserved. Published in the United States by David Fickling
Books, an imprint of Random House Children's Books,
a division of Random House, Inc., New York.
Originally published in Great Britain by Doubleday,
an imprint of Random House Children's Books,
a division of the Random House Group Ltd., London, in 2008.

David Fickling Books and the colophon are trademarks of David Fickling.

Visit us on the Web! www.randomhouse.com/kids

Educators and librarians, for a variety of teaching tools,
visit us at www.randomhouse.com/teachers

Library of Congress Cataloging-in-Publication Data
is available upon request.
ISBN 978-0-385-75131-5 (trade) — ISBN 978-0-385-75132-2 (lib. bdg.)
— ISBN 978-0-375-89536-4 (e-book)

Printed in the United States of America
March 2010
10   9   8   7   6   5   4   3   2   1

First American Edition
Random House Children's Books supports the First Amendment
and celebrates the right to read.

For Stephen – P.S.
For Jack – C.R.

CHAPTER 1

I have heard people exclaim that they'd be better off dead – weary washerwomen on a midnight shift in the steam cellars, ragged beggars down by the Temple Bar, fine young ladies snubbed at a Hightown ball . . . But if they had seen what I saw on that cold and foggy night, they would have realized the foolishness of their words.

It was a sight that will haunt me till my dying day – after which, I fervently hope and pray, I shall remain undisturbed.

This was not something that could be said for the ghastly apparitions that stumbled through the swirling mists towards me. Some lurched haltingly, their arms dangling at their sides; others had their hands outstretched before them, as though their bony fingertips rather than their sunken eyes were guiding their lurching bodies through the curdled fog.

There was a wizened hag with a hooked nose and rat's-nest hair. A portly matron, the ague that had seen her off still glistening on her furrowed brow . . . A sly-eyed ragger and a bare-knuckled wrestler, his left eyeball out of its socket and dangling on a glistening thread. A corpulent costermonger; a stooped scrivener, their clothes – one satins and frill, the other threadbare serge – smeared alike with black mud and sewer slime. A maid, a chimney-sweep, a couple of stable-lads; one with the side of his skull stoved in by a single blow from a horse's hoof, the other grey and glittery-eyed from the blood-flecked cough that had ended his life. And a burly river-tough – his fine waistcoat in tatters and his chin tattoo obscured by filth. Glistening at his neck was the deep wound that had taken him from this world to the next.

I shrank back in horror and pressed hard against the cool white marble of the de Vere family vault at my back. Beside me – his body quivering like a slab of jellied ham – Sir Alfred was breathing in stuttering, wheezy gasps. From three sides of the marble tomb in that fog-filled graveyard, the serried ranks of the undead were forming up in a grotesque parody of a parade-ground drill.

'They've found me,' the old doctor croaked, in a voice not much more than a whisper.

I followed his terrified gaze and found myself staring at four ragged figures in military uniform, red jackets with gold braid at the epaulettes and cuffs, who were standing on a flat-topped tomb above the massed ranks. Each of them bore the evidence of fatal injuries.

The terrible gash down the face of one, that

Each of them bore the evidence of fatal injuries.

had left his cheekbone exposed and a flap of leathery skin dangling. The blood-stained chest and jagged stump – all that remained of his left arm – of the second figure, splinters of yellow bone protruding through the wreaths of grimy bandages. The rusting axe, cleaving the battered bell-top shako, which was embedded in the skull of the third. And the bulging bloodshot eyes of the fourth, the frayed length of rough rope that had strangulated his last breath still hanging round his bruised and red-raw neck – and a flagpole clutched in his gnarled hands.

As I watched, he raised the splintered flagpole high. Gripping my swordstick, I stared at the fluttering curtain of blood-stained cloth, tasselled brocade hanging in filthy matted strands along the four sides. At its centre was the embroidered regimental emblem – the Angel of Victory, her wings spread wide on a sky-blue field, and beneath, the words *33rd Regiment of Foot* written in an angular italic script. The ghastly standard-bearer's tight lips parted to reveal a row of blackened teeth.

'Fighting Thirty-Third!' he cried out, his voice a rasping whisper.

The corpses swayed where they stood, their bony arms reaching forward, with tattered sleeves hanging limply in the foggy air. I smelled the sourness of the sewers about them; that, and the sweet whiff of death. Their sunken eyes bored into mine.

We were surrounded. There was nothing Sir Alfred or I could do. The standard-bearer's voice echoed hoarsely round the graveyard.

'Advance!'

CHAPTER 2

In my line of work, I've encountered my fair share of restless spirits from beyond the grave. There was Madame Lavinia's poltergeist, who terrorized the thrill-seeking guests at her tea parties. And Pastor Shakemaple's Iroquois spirit guide, with a taste for cheap whiskey and expensive jewellery. And of course the late Mercy Hornby, queen of the phantasmal plane, who was on intimate terms with three Roman emperors and Alexander the Great – extraordinary apparitions, each and every one of them . . .

Unfortunately, Madame Lavinia's apparition was more piano wire than poltergeist, and Shakemaple's clerical robes concealed a magic lantern and a pair of sticky fingers. As for the ghost of Mercy Hornby; she was no more than a shop dummy in a shroud, operated by a music-hall ventriloquist in search of a new career.

I should know, because I played a part in unmasking them. Ha'penny fraudsters, the lot of them, out to fleece the gullible. But what I encountered in that graveyard on that moonlit night was no cheap illusion. No wires, no lanterns or cheap theatrical tricks had conjured up the legion of the dead.

The truth was far worse . . .

It all began on a crisp autumn morning, the sky the colour of an Indian Runner duck egg. I'm a tick-tock lad by trade. My job is to deliver things all over the city – anything, from a dusty writ or a document in need of a signature to the boxed consignment of giant African snails that I'd dropped off only the day before at the exclusive Culloden Club for their annual members-only mollusc race. I'm quick and efficient, highstacking over the rooftops of the city as fast as I can because – tick-tock! – time is money. Some jobs – like the snails – are one-offs, while others are more regular and, since it was the second Wednesday in the month, I had an appointment with one Cornelius Frimley of *Frimley's Funereal Supplies and Grave Chandlery*.

I was running late that morning and had to be quick, but I also had to be careful. Although the sun was shining, treacherous traces of frost still lingered in the shadows, threatening to turn my ankle or make me skid. At the Mansion House, a tricky Striding Edge manoeuvre and a moment of carelessness almost pitched me over the side of a crumbling parapet.

On such a glorious morning though, with the sun shining, a light breeze blowing and the city air as clear as it ever gets, nothing could dent my spirits. And, though you need a head for heights and a steady nerve, there is nothing as exhilarating as highstacking. Leaping, rolling and running across the roof-tops – plinth to pediment, gargoyle to gable – the experienced highstacker can race across the city, while the streets below are snarled with slow-moving traffic.

I made quick progress, and at five to nine the imposing brown-brick building, with its white stone window arches and fluted pilasters, that housed *Frimley's Funereal Supplies and Grave Chandlery*, loomed up before me. At nine o'clock on the dot, I was standing outside Cornelius Frimley's office. I rapped on the door.

'Come in,' came a thin, wheezing voice, and I entered the room.

Cornelius Frimley was seated at the desk before me, his fingers buried in a drift of paperwork. He raised his head wearily, a frown on his pallid brow. 'Ah, Barnaby,' he said.

The steel-rimmed spectacles he wore were so strong, it looked as though his huge, magnified eyes had been lifted from his face and glued to the inside of the lenses. Bright red veins lined the glowing yellowed eyeballs. In contrast, his face in the flickering light was as pale as the wax candle that cast it, and made all the more ghostly by the deep dark circles under each eye.

From the look of him, the poor chap never saw sunlight from one end of the day to the other. Despite its outer appearance of grandeur, inside, the brown-brick building had been transformed into a warren of winding corridors and tiny offices. Cornelius Frimley's office was little more than a broom-cupboard. There wasn't even a window.

'Prompt as ever,' he wheezed, peering round the flickering candle that stood before him. He chuckled. 'I'd ask you to sit, but . . .'

It was his little joke. The tiny room was furnished with a large varnished cabinet and a rolltop desk, behind which, Cornelius Frimley had managed to insert an ancient high-backed leather chair. In the remaining space, it was standing-room only, and we both knew it. I smiled.

'Something has just come in, Barnaby,' he said, those huge eyes of his staring at me unblinkingly. 'A matter of some urgency.'

He pushed back his chair and turned towards the cabinet behind him. As tall as it was broad, the yellowed oak cabinet took up half the office. It was comprised of dozens of small bone-handled drawers. Pausing for a moment, Cornelius Frimley stared at them, his narrow shoulders hunched forward. Then he crouched down, his knees clicking like snapped twigs as he did so, and unlocked one of the drawers.

'Here we are,' he said, turning and placing a box, about the size of a house-brick, on the table in front of me. It jangled slightly as he did so. 'Links,' he said.

'Links?'

'Links for a finger-chain.' He flapped his hands about airily. 'My best chainsmith is waiting for them – Ada Gussage, 17 Adelaide Mansions . . .'

Finger-chains were the very latest in funeral fashion. No well-to-do deceased would be seen dead without one! They were attached to the forefinger of the corpse at one end and a bell at the other, so that anyone unfortunate enough to awaken in the coffin could summon help and be dug up.

'Adelaide Mansions,' I repeated and frowned. To my knowledge, there were two Adelaide Mansions in the city. One was situated on salubrious Gallup Row in the best part of town; the other . . .

'Gatling Quays,' said Cornelius Frimley, and my heart sank.

Gatling Quays. As a rule, it was a place I liked to avoid. Situated between riverside East Bank, with its scratting mudlarks and tattooed toughs, and the port of Riverhythe, where incoming ships would dock, Gatling Quays was worse than either. Its cobbled streets were lined with vast warehouses, where the cargo from foreign shores was stored before being distributed to the factories, mills and workshops of the city. The wealth of goods and materials piled up there attracted harbour-toughs and skim-merchants to the quays like lice to a workhouse blanket.

'As quickly as you can, Barnaby,' Cornelius Frimley urged me. 'Ada needs those links for an important client down there in the quays.'

He shook my hand – a cold, damp experience, like squeezing a raw fish – and slumped back onto his leather chair. I stepped to the door, slipping the heavy box into the inside pocket of my coat.

'And tell Ada the finger-chain has to be ready by tomorrow. The client's people will be around to collect it first thing.'

Promising I would, I left the room, the sound of rustling paper filling the air as Cornelius Frimley dived back into his mound of invoices, orders and dockets. The door clicked shut behind me.

I left the building through the first window I came to on the maze-like sixth-floor corridor, edged along the glistening window-ledge and shinned up an ornate cast-iron drainpipe to the roof above.

As I made my way to Gatling Quays, the rooftops of the city districts lay spread out before me. Hightown, the Theatre District, the Wasps' Nest . . . I highstacked fast and, as I did so, I thanked my lucky stars that I wasn't locked up inside a windowless broom-cupboard of an office, hour after endless hour.

Mind you, even an airless office had its attractions compared to Gatling Quays. Down among the warehouses, you had to watch your step. Every alley, quayside and corner was controlled by a petty skim-merchant and his crew of toughs, looking to cream off a percentage of the goods from the passing wagons. The Bevan Street Crew, the Flour Bag Mob, the Harness Riggers, the Tallow Gang . . . There were a dozen of them in all, each one running their own protection rackets – and prepared to defend their small patch of cobbles, or 'homestones', to the death.

As I neared my destination, the air grew thicker, with a thick fish-stew fog from the docklands drifting upriver to the quays. I found myself in the middle of a dense swirling blanket that stank of brackish seaweed and coal smoke, and hung in the air, blotting out the sun. I took a moment to orientate myself.

Seething Lane, I was looking for. Adelaide Mansions; number 17.

With the swirling fog, it wasn't easy. But I didn't want to get lost. In and out, as fast as a ferret down a fat farmer's breeches, that was the best way to visit Gatling Quays. A clock at the top of a distant church tower tolled the hour.

Eleven o'clock, I noted, relieved.

As a rule, the mornings were comparatively quiet in the quays, with the crews sleeping in after their night-time activities. All the same, I had no intention of making my visit to the quays any longer than necessary . . .

I recognized a square chimney to my right, lancing the dense air. That was my landmark. Perched on the top of the long corrugated roof of Barnard's flour warehouse, the tall chimney had graced the skyline of Gatling Quays for as long as I could remember. Below it, a constantly burning furnace kept the stacks of flour in the warehouse dry. My grand-sounding destination – Adelaide Mansions; a five-storey tenement building that housed many of the local warehouse workers – stood on the corner close by.

Keeping the fuzzy chimney in my sights, I made my way gingerly across the pitched roof of a timber merchant's, the cracked tiles slipping beneath my feet, threatening to pitch me down into the log piles in the yard below. At the end, I ran the length of a parapet wall as fast as I dared, before throwing myself into a Running Grapple.

Not for the novice, this particular manoeuvre. The Running Grapple is used when the building being jumped *to* is higher than the one being jumped *from*. The high-stacker must leap up, pedal his legs as he flies through the air, then hook his fingers over the parapet and – legs still pedalling – 'run' up the wall.

As I reached the top of the tall, windowless warehouse, I paused for a moment to catch my breath, before pigeon-stepping along a narrower ridge and out onto a curved buttress. There I stopped again, and looked down. The back of the tenement block was the next building on my right. It looked neglected, with half the windows boarded up, rusting fire escapes peeling from the walls and wilting sprays of buddleia sprouting from the crumbling brickwork. I found myself wondering whether Cornelius Frimley had got the address right.

There was only one way to find out.

Stepping back, I readied myself for a tricky Flying Fox manoeuvre. A twelve-step run up was the optimum. I had three. Springing forward as best I could, I launched myself into the air – arms outstretched and the corners of my jacket gripped between my fingertips – and soared across the yawning void below me. Seconds later, I landed squarely on a jutting ledge, barely three inches wide, and regained my balance.

I dusted myself down. I needed to be quick. The sooner I dropped off my parcel and left the quays, the better.

There was a door at the centre of the flat roof. It was locked, but when I shook it, the whole lot came away in my hands. I went inside and gagged at the foul odour – a mixture of musty vermin and sour onions. As I headed down the rubbish-strewn stairs, it suddenly occurred to me that something was wrong.

Normally, a block such as this would be stuffed to the gills with tenants. Adelaide Mansions, though, was deserted and, but for the sound of my own footfalls echoing round the stairwell, silent as the grave. Doors to the apartments on every floor were open or off their hinges, revealing the detritus of abandoned family lives inside. It wasn't until I arrived on the second floor that I came to my first closed door.

Number 17.

I went to put my ear to the cracked wooden panel, to hear a faint *tap-tap-tap* sound coming from deep inside the apartment. I knocked at the door. The tapping stopped and heavy footsteps approached. The next moment, the door flew open and I found myself confronted by a vast barrel of a woman in a shapeless floral dress. Old and red-faced, legs like tree trunks and forearms like giant hams, she looked at me through currant-bun eyes, her fingernails raking back her wiry grey hair.

'Ada Gussage?' I said, reaching inside my pocket.

The woman folded her arms. 'The same,' she said revealing a row of stubby yellow teeth. 'And you are?'

'Barnaby Grimes,' I said, holding out the small parcel. 'This is for you.'

'Oh, thank heavens for that,' she said at the sight of it. Her face creased into a happy smile and those currant-bun eyes of hers twinkled as she reached out and took the parcel. She shook it, making the contents inside jangle softly. Then, unknotting the piece of string tied round it, she eased off the lid and looked inside.

'Seems about right,' she mused, shaking the box. 'Enough for a ten-footer, with a few links to spare . . .'

I peered down into the box. It was full of small brass ovals waiting to be joined together to form a chain, with a tap of a hammer and a squeeze of pliers. Also in the box, nestling amongst the links, were two larger metal rings.

'Mr Frimley said that the finger-chain has to be ready by tomorrow,' I said, remembering his words. 'The client's people will be around to collect it first thing.'

'I'm sure they will, dearie,' Ada Gussage said, pushing the lid of the box back into place. 'I'm sure they will. These days, nobody wants to be buried without a finger-chain, now do they?'

I shook my head.

'And they knows where to find me. After

all, I'm the only one left in the mansions since the hauntings began . . .'

'Hauntings?' I said, intrigued.

'Ghosts, they say, just over yonder in the graveyard by Gatling Sump,' she said, and her eyes sparkled. 'Wandering about in the river fog at dusk, scaring folk witless.' She shook her head, the wiry hair trembling. 'But I'm used to death in my trade, and it'll take more than a few phantoms in red coats to make Ada Gussage leave the mansion, make no mistake.' She shot me a yellow smile. 'But never mind all that,' she said, 'would you care for a cup of tea – a lovely smoked Assam, fresh from a clipper just docked last week?'

She stepped back and her fluttering hand beckoned me in. I looked down the narrow corridor to the parlour at the other end. Even though it was approaching midday, a lamp was lit, casting a golden light onto a small table, its surface covered with the tools of her strange trade – hammers, pliers, a soldering-iron and small anvil.

'That's very nice of you,' I said, 'but I'd best be going.' I added cheerfully, 'I've got lots to do and you know what they say – tick-tock, time is money.'

'In that case, Mr Grimes, I'll let you to.' She jangled the box in her hands and smiled. 'When you see him, tell Mr Frimley not to worry. Ada Gussage won't let him down!'

I tipped my hat and bade her good day.

'Goodbye, Barnaby,' said Ada Gussage, stepping back into her apartment. 'And take care out there on the cobbles.'

'Oh, I shall, I shall,' I assured her as I took my leave – though I had no intention of setting foot on the cobblestone streets of Gatling Quays.

On the fourth-floor landing, I disturbed a mangy ginger tom, that yowled indignantly and tore past me, puffs of dust thrown up into the shafts of light in its wake.

*

Back on the rooftop, the air had cleared. Setting off, I quickly left the neglected building behind me and was just getting into my stack-hopping stride over the chimneys, when I heard the sound of angry shouting from somewhere below. Stopping for a moment, I peered down over the edge of a rooftop, to see three great hoodlums clustered together in a triangle on the cobblestones below. They were dwarfing a fourth person, who was cowering in the middle.

'These are *our* homestones, and *you're* trespassing,' one of the ruffians growled, thrusting his brutal features into the frightened individual's face.

'Looks like we've trapped a rat, Lol,' said the second with a snarl.

'And you know what we do with rats, don't you?' said the third, and there was a flash of metal as he pulled a knife from his belt.

The others did the same.

My stomach churned. Even though I was high up, from the tassel-sleeved overcoats that this lot were wearing, they looked to me like members of the Ratcatchers Crew. If I was right, I didn't fancy the chances of the poor sap they'd just fingered.

At that moment, the said sap turned round to face the third of his thuggish tormentors. His clothes were more tattered than I remembered and his hair was much shorter, but I knew him at once.

His name was Will Farmer.

Like me, he was a tick-tock lad. But there the similarity ended. I was a highstacker; he was a cobblestone-creeper, stuck down on the ground. But he had spirit and ambition, and wanted to take to the rooftops like yours truly. I liked him and had promised to give him a couple of highstacking lessons when I had some spare time. That had been months ago, and I still hadn't got round to it. If I had,

I realized, then perhaps Will wouldn't be where he was now.

'Go on, stick him, Lol!' one of the ruffians snarled.

Without a second thought, I dropped down over the guttering and performed a speedy Drainpipe Sluice – praying the whole lot wasn't about to come away from the wall – and landed with a slapped thud feet away from the three ruffians and their hapless victim. The Ratcatchers spun round, weapons raised.

I drew my sword.

They were on me in an instant. I lunged forward, knocking the dagger out of the first ruffian's hand and sending it scudding across the road. Then I parried a blow from the second, before spinning round and pinning him up against the wall, the point of my sword pressed against the base of his throat.

Behind me, the heftiest of the three thugs bellowed furiously, 'Let him go!'

They were on me in an instant.

I turned to confront him, only to find that he'd grabbed Will and had his own knife pressed at the lad's neck.

It was at that moment I realized Will Farmer wasn't the only one I recognized. The thug before me was none other than Thump McConnell, skim-merchant and leader of the Ratcatchers.

Our paths had crossed a year earlier. I'd inadvertently helped him out of a scrape when a consignment of pungent spices I'd been delivering to the kitchens of Admiral McMahone had thrown the dogs of the Harbour Constabulary off his scent and allowed Thump to escape across the rooftops. At the time, he'd told me that he owed me one. It was time to call in that favour.

'Thump McConnell,' I said.

I saw him frown, the knife still pressed at Will's neck. His two henchmen looked at him, puzzled. All three of them were wearing Ratcatcher clothes; black breeches, flat hard-peak caps and short overcoats made from a patchwork of rat skins, the sleeves fringed with leathery tails.

'Do I know you?' he demanded, his gruff voice showing no sign of recognition.

'Red madras curry powder,' I said. 'Last year on the Admiral's roof. Pack of sneezing bull mastiffs in the courtyard and you on the roof with a sackful of silver plate. Ring any bells?'

Thump frowned. 'Last year?' he said, the rats' tails on his coat sleeves swinging as he scratched his ear.

Slow on the uptake was old Thump. Too many blows to the head in the bare-knuckled fights where he'd earned his nickname. But slowly, the light dawned.

'Not the tick-tock lad . . . ?' He smiled slowly. 'The one who helped me down the guttering . . . Benjamin, is it?'

'Barnaby,' I corrected him.

'Barnaby!' he agreed, switching his knife

from right hand to left and sticking out a great paw of a hand. 'Barnaby Grimes! I owe you one for that night, and no mistake.'

Sheathing my sword, I turned and shook the paw – my smile glazing on my face as my knuckles cracked. I nodded to Will, who was still in Thump's knife-wielding grasp.

'And this is a friend of mine,' I added, taking back my hand and thrusting it safely into my pocket. 'Will Farmer.'

'Friend, you say?' said Thump, looking down at Will, who was staring at me like a lapdog at a lost owner.

Abruptly, Thump let him go and re-sheathed his own blade. Will stumbled across the cobbles and stood beside me. The other two stepped menacingly towards us.

'It's all right Lol, Mugsy,' Thump told them. 'Leave 'em be.' He looked at me, then Will; then, with a flourish, he reached into the pocket of his rat-skin jerkin and pulled out a fob-watch on a chain. He flicked open the embossed silver cover and peered at the hands. 'It's ten after midday,' he said, looking at his crew. 'The truce has started.'

'Truce?' I said.

He turned to me. 'Haven't you heard?' he said. 'A forty-eight hour truce has been agreed between all the quays' gangs. As a mark of respect.'

I looked around and noticed that the streets of Gatling Quays did look unnaturally quiet, even for midday.

'The Emperor's being buried tomorrow,' said Thump grimly. 'The twelve gangs had a big meet last night, and I was elected the new Emperor of Gatling Quays. It's down to me to give old Firejaw a proper sendoff, with all the trimmings.'

Firejaw O'Rourke – or the Emperor of Gatling Quays as he was usually known – was the most powerful of the skim-merchants. For years, the Emperor's crew, the Sumpside Boys, had run the biggest protection racket of them all, skimming a percentage off every major business in the quays – and woe betide anyone who failed to cough up. Six foot six, and with a beard of flaming red, Firejaw O'Rourke cut quite a figure, even among the hardened gangs of the quays.

With his untimely death, the gangs had been thrown into disarray, with the leaders of all the gangs vying amongst themselves to be the new Emperor. Thump McConnell of the Ratcatchers had obviously come out on top. The leaders of the other gangs – Flob McManus of the Flour Bag Mob or Lenny Dempster, O'Rourke's successor with the Sumpside Boys, for instance – were probably less than happy about it. Old Thump would have to earn their respect, and a successful sendoff for Firejaw would be a good start.

'Nasty accident,' Thump was saying, his thin lips taut. 'Boatload of fireworks and a stubbed-out cigar . . .' He shook his head grimly. 'Half burned when they fished 'im out of the water. Not a pretty sight.' Thump McConnell's eyes narrowed. 'I take it you'll be there to pay your respects, Barnaby Grimes,' he said, and from his steely glare I knew I wasn't being given a choice. 'The funeral's at the Adelaide Graveyard, down by the sump . . .'

As he uttered the name, I saw his two henchmen flinch and exchange glances. The one called Lol swallowed noisily. Thump McConnell rounded on him furiously and slapped him hard across the face with the back of his hand, the rats'-tails fringed sleeve lashing his cheek.

'If I hear one more word about phantoms and ghosts, and ghouls in red jackets, it'll be your last. D'you understand? Truce or no truce!'

'Didn't say nuffin',' Lol muttered, tracing his fingers gingerly down the welts on his face, the raw lines where the rats' tails had lashed him beaded with blood.

'Didn't need to,' said Thump, and wagged his finger. 'Just you make sure you don't.' He turned back to me, and continued speaking as though nothing had happened. 'Now that I'm taking over as the new ganglord, it's my job to make sure the funeral runs like greased clockwork. All the skim-merchants and their crews will be there, along with well-wishers . . .' His face contorted into a thin-lipped smile, menacing and humour-free. 'Such as yourself, Barnaby, and your friend here.'

'I wouldn't miss it,' I answered.

'Good.' He nodded sternly, then turned to the others. 'Come on, lads,' he said, 'there's still that little matter with the Fetter Lane Scroggers to attend to . . .'

With that, the three of them turned and left. Will and I watched them go – bulky Thump McConnell in the middle, flanked by his two heavies; the three of them swaying to the left and right in unison.

Will Farmer turned to me. 'Oh, Mr Grimes,'

he said, 'thank you, thank you. I was meant to be delivering a wagon permit when—'

'Call me Barnaby,' I told him. 'Wagon permits! That's a job for a dozen harbour constables, not a lone tick-tock lad.'

'But the desk sergeant said it would be easy . . .' Will began.

'Yes, well, best choose your jobs a bit more carefully in future, Will. Still, no harm done.' I clapped a hand on his shoulder. 'Let's get out of here.'

'The sooner the better,' said Will, turning on his heels and heading for the drainpipe I'd shinned down.

'Hey, where do you think you're going?' I called.

He stopped in his tracks. 'I thought . . .' He frowned. 'You did mean it, didn't you?' he said. 'When you said you'd show me how to highstack?'

I laughed. The kid was nothing if not enthusiastic.

'Course I did, Will,' I said, 'but let's not try to run before we can walk, eh? Besides, we're going to have to put that lesson on hold for a little while longer,' I told him. 'You and me have got a funeral to go to.'

CHAPTER 3

'Balance, Will. It's all a matter of balance,' I reminded him the next day, calling across from the flat roof I was standing on, to the jutting pedestal behind me where young Will Farmer was still poised, his legs shaking and his face taut and pale. 'Relax and lean into the jump,' I said. 'Don't think about the drop. Concentrate on the landing . . .'

He looked across the gaping chasm at me and nodded earnestly, his cheeks flexing as he clenched his teeth. He squared his stance and raised his arms. The low sun cast a long, cross-like shadow behind him.

'That's the way,' I told him encouragingly.

Normally, highstacking across town to Gatling Quays would have taken me an hour and a half at the very outside. I'd allowed twice that amount of time to shepherd Will across the rooftops, taking a long and convoluted route that avoided the need for any particularly tricky manoeuvres.

If not a born highstacker, Will Farmer was certainly a quick learner, swiftly mastering the Tuppenny Step and Two-Trick Pony, and proving himself a dab hand at stack-hopping. Now, however, perched on the edge of the jutting stone some seventy feet above the teeming street below, his nerve had gone.

'All right,' I said. 'You know what to do. Push yourself off. Keep your arms outstretched. Then, when you land, roll forwards . . .'

'Rather than tipping backwards,' Will muttered, rubbing a hand over his cropped hair.

He took a deep breath and leaned back on his left foot. Then, with look of grim concentration, he kicked off from the wall and thrust himself into the air. As he hurtled towards me, I stepped to one side and readied myself to support him if he stumbled. A moment later he landed like an albatross on an iceberg and clattered into a sideways roll, before colliding with the parapet at the far end of the flat roof.

'Not the most elegant Peabody Roll,' I said, helping Will to his feet and dusting him off, 'but I think you're getting the feel for it.'

'Do you really think so?' said Will, now enthusiastic again after his bout of nerves. 'Can I try another?'

'Just follow me,' I said. 'We'll ridge-walk the rest of the way.'

We continued, me in front, Will following behind, copying every move I made. The bright sun cast deep shadows that made every brick, every ridge, every stanchion and pediment stand out clearly, while the gentle breeze that morning was not enough to cause any of the dangerous eddies and currents that so often swirled round the rooftops, plucking at those daring enough to be up on them. In short, it was a perfect day for high-stacking – and a perfect day for a funeral.

Strains of music – bagpipes, a trumpet, a drum – were the first indication that we were approaching our destination. Sure enough, at the end of the long pitched roof of a tenement block, the pair of us looked down to see a small square – Angel Place – crowded with a great throng of milling people. Members of the Gatling Quays' gangs clustered together in whispering groups. From above, the makeshift uniforms worn by the different crews made a constantly changing patchwork of colours.

'We're in time,' I said. 'Thank goodness.'

'How are we going to get down?' said Will excitedly. 'A Drainpipe Sluice? Or how about a Salmon's Drop?'

I smiled. 'Best to arrive in one piece,' I said, and nodded towards a zigzag framework of cast-iron stairs, painted brick red, that had been bolted to the back wall of the building. 'We'll take the easy way down.'

'All right,' Will said, his voice a mixture of disappointment and relief.

He lowered himself agilely down to the top landing and, gripping the rusting banister, clopped down the flights. I followed him. The sunlight glinted on his scalp.

'Looks like you've had a close shave,' I laughed.

Will looked round. 'That Peabody Roll?' he asked.

'No, your haircut,' I said.

He grinned back at me, his right hand shooting to his head. 'Not exactly,' he said, with a grimace. 'I sold my hair to a wigmaker last week to make up the rent on my half room in the Wasps' Nest.'

'Are times that hard?' I asked.

Will nodded. 'I'm a cobblestone-creeper, not a highstacker like you,' he explained. 'I can't charge highstacking rates.'

'Then we'll just have to do something about that,' I said. 'Now, let's get this over with.'

At the bottom landing, instead of lowering the final length of ladder, I swung down on a horizontal strut and dropped lightly to the cobblestones below me. Will landed beside me a moment later.

''Ere, what's your game?' came a gruff voice over the sound of the music, dirge-like with its droning bagpipes and thudding drum.

I turned to find myself being confronted by half a dozen toughs. Their leader, a hefty brawler with thick, slicked-back hair and a wide-brimmed Kempton, stepped forward. There were smudges of flour on his hard face and brawny tattooed arms, which he folded as he eyed me and Will up and down. Like the crew at his shoulders, he wore a loose-fitting sleeveless jacket over his shirt, fashioned from flour sacks and decorated with skulls daubed in black tar. These, I realized, must be the Flour Bag Mob.

'We've come to pay our respects to the Emperor,' I said simply, removing my coal-stack hat and clicking it shut.

'And who might you be?' he demanded, thrusting his grim, lumpen face into my own.

'He's with me,' said Thump McConnell, barging his way through the gathering and placing a heavy arm round mine and Will's shoulders. 'Come on, lads,' he said. 'Today, you're honorary Ratcatchers. You march with us.'

Leaving the leader of the Flour Bag Mob staring after us, dumbfounded, Thump ushered the two of us across the square. The music grew louder. I looked at the band more closely.

The drummer and bagpipes players were both hefty, the brass buttons of their tartan jackets straining at their chests. The trumpeter, in contrast, was a scrawny individual with a long scar that extended from the corner of his mouth to the bottom of his left ear and made it look as though he was grinning lopsidedly, despite his puckered lips. The final member of the quartet was a backwards cellist, playing the great fiddle strapped to his back by reaching behind with long thin dextrous arms; one hand behind his neck, the other sawing behind the small of his back with a bow.

All four wore feathered Highland shakos and black kilts, and stamped their heavy boots in time to the low, sonorous funeral songs they played. They were a professional dirge band, expert at providing a mournful musical backdrop to the proceedings.

I recognized an old music-hall song about a saloon girl called Daisy Monroe in amongst them, much slower than the original, but with the tune intact. I guessed that it must have been one of the Emperor's favourites, and was about to say as much to Will when a black hearse drew up.

Will looked impressed, and I could see why. Resting at the back of the black and gold carriage, every inch of it decorated with orange, yellow and purple chrysanthemums, drawn by a pair of jet black stallions, sprays of ostrich plumes fixed to their heads, was one of the grandest coffins I had ever seen. It was made from highly polished oak, furnished with solid-gold handles and crowned with vast bouquets of roses and lilies, their petals trembling as the horses danced about on the spot. The young driver – his black suit a couple of sizes too large for his bony frame – had pushed back his top hat and was watching Thump McConnell keenly, waiting for his nod to flick the reins and spur the horses into action.

'They do things in style down here in the quays,' I murmured to Will.

He frowned. 'But where's his family?' he asked. 'His wife? His children?'

'As far as I know, *this* was his family,' I told him, with a broad sweep of my arm.

All twelve of the district gangs were here; the Ratcatchers, the Flour Bag Mob, the Bevan Street Crew, the Harness Riggers, the Tallow Gang, the Lampblackers, the Pressers, the Joinery Blades, the Barrel Boys, the Fetter Lane Scroggers, the Spike-Tooth Smilers and, last but not least, the formidable Sumpside Boys. All were under strictest orders to remain on their best behaviour, and the atmosphere was as brittle as a duchess's smile. No gang leader wanted to be slighted or disrespected; no one wanted to lose face. Stewards with black armbands were passing between the crowd, organizing them into the ranks that they would take as they marched from Angel Square, through the narrow

All twelve of the district gangs were here.

streets of Gatling Quays, to Adelaide Graveyard.

Finally, with the dirge band at the front, the funeral carriage immediately behind, surrounded by the Sumpside Boys in their ankle-length bearskin coats and straw boat-caps, we were just about to set off, when there was the sound of raised voices behind us. I looked round. Two stewards – elderly members of the lowly Pressers gang – were patting the air, trying to calm the situation down, but neither the leader of the Harness Riggers, in his brass-buckled leather over-coat, nor his portly opposite number in the Barrel Boys – the gold threads of his embroi-dered waistcoat glinting in the sunlight – were having any of it.

'This is out of order,' the leader of the Harness Riggers was snarling. 'Third most powerful gang in the quays and we're dumped all the way back here . . .'

'Bunch of prancing ponies, the lot of you,'

the leader of the Barrel Boys shot back, punctuating each word with a stab of his finger. 'The Barrel Boys were skimming ale wagons when you lot were still in stained knee-breeches.'

'One second,' said Thump McConnell, tapping the drummer on his shoulder.

The drummer nodded without missing a beat on the great drum that was strung round his shoulders and hung, vertically, at his chest. Strolling back along the line, his huge bulk cutting a swathe through the ranks of hoodlums, Thump approached the two furious gang leaders. There was a smile on his lips, but I noticed the vicious glint in his eyes as he leaned towards them.

'Not now, lads,' he said quietly. 'Not today. Have you forgotten about the truce?' The smile grew broader, even as his eyes narrowed. 'I want you to be nice to one another.' He raised his two great hams of hands and placed them on the back of the two leaders' heads.

Then, with a grunt of exertion – and maintaining that sinister smile of his – he shoved the two heads hard together. There was a loud *crack*! and, with a muffled groan, the two gang leaders crumpled to the ground. 'And show some respect!' Thump snarled.

Back at the front of the line once more, the drum now silent, Thump McConnell and five other Ratcatcher gang members chosen to be pallbearers, stood on one side of the carriage, while six enormous Sumpside Boys stood on the other. Two emaciated-looking young lads provided by *Frimley's Funereal Supplies* – their pale faces set with the solemnity of the occasion – stood beside them. The rest of us stood behind, with the other gangs of Gatling Quays, in ordered ranks. The cellist, trumpeter and bagpipes player fell silent. The drummer raised his arms, the creamy felt-covered heads of his drumsticks quivering in the air for a moment, then . . .

B-bang!

He struck the two sides of the drum once more, a resounding thud that brought everyone to attention. The trumpet and pipes started up a new tune; the carriage driver cracked his whip and the whole dismal parade lurched forwards. As we marched through the shadowy streets, windows were flung open all about us, and scrawny children and grey-haired matrons leaned out, their heads bowed in respect. Crowds of people gushed from the front doors, their hands filled with flowers, which they tossed at the passing carriage – carnations, gladioli, garlands of Michaelmas daisies . . .

Thump turned to me as we rounded the corner onto the Belvedere Mile, the broadest avenue of Gatling Quays, thicker crowds than ever greeting our passing by. The carriage, already half-hidden beneath a mountain of blooms, clattered softly over a carpet of still more flowers that littered our route.

'A good turn out,' he said, his eyes moist with emotion.

'He was a well-respected man,' I said, choosing my words carefully.

Thump nodded, satisfied, and turned back again.

At the end of the avenue, the road divided into two narrower roads. The left-hand fork led down to the mudflats and jetties; the right, along to Riverhythe. Between the two, the dark green of its gnarled yew trees speckled with waxy blood-red berries, was Adelaide Graveyard, black cast-iron railings separating it from the roads on either side. We marched on between the throngs of bystanders towards the arched entrance, its tall and ornately forged gates decorated with lions and lambs, and came to a halt.

I glanced up at the deserted Adelaide Mansions opposite. There was no sign of Ada Gussage at any of its many windows.

At Thump McConnell's signal, the five

other pallbearers – each one as tall as him, though none quite as bulky – pulled off their flat caps and seized the edge of the coffin. On the other side of the carriage, the Sumpside Boys did the same. Then, having lifted it off the bier, they gripped a gold handle each with a great fist and hefted the coffin up onto their shoulders. From their grunts and sighs, it was clear that the coffin was as heavy as it looked. The music grew quieter till all that was left was the slow rhythmic *thump-thump-thump* of the drum.

All round, the bystanders fell still. Then, guided by the sombre beat, we fell into step once more, passed beneath the archway and on into the graveyard.

It was a mournful place, without a doubt. There was a low, swirling mist snaking its way around our legs, and the bottle-green yew trees rustled softly, muffling the air and shutting out the sun – and making the hairs at the nape of my neck stand on end.

I wasn't the only one to feel ill at ease. The ranks of mourners behind me seemed just as troubled. Several of them were looking anxiously about them, glancing over their shoulders or craning their necks as they peered nervously into the shadows between the trees. A member of the Lampblackers crew, the characteristic ring of candles round the broad brim of his barrel-hat flickering, suddenly started back, his teeth bared with fear – before gathering himself self-consciously. A Tallow Gang member pulled a yellow handkerchief from the pocket of his high-buttoned waxed acton and patted it to his brow.

Then I noticed Lol – the tough who had challenged me and Will the previous day. Our gaze met, and I saw that his eyes were filled with terror.

'This place makes my skin crawl,' I heard Will whisper.

'Me too, Will,' I whispered back. 'And *they*

don't like it either,' I added, nodding back at the two stallions at the gate, who were pawing the ground and whinnying nervously as the hapless carriage driver struggled to keep them from bolting.

The stewards, meanwhile, were darting between us, giving instructions. We took our places round the grave in a wide circle, the twelve gangs forming themselves into a dozen narrow wedges, like the five-minute sections of a great clock. Will and I stood with the Ratcatchers, our coalstack hats clutched in our hands, directly behind the vast marble headstone, which was fresh from the stonecutter's yard, chiselled and polished that very morning. It marked the Emperor's last resting place. Before us stood the vicar, nodding to each of the mourners in turn as they arrived.

The Reverend Simeon Spool was his name. He was a stooped and desiccated individual with thin, flaxen hair, parted low on one side, and that bounced up and down on his head like a square of plaited straw every time he nodded. From what I'd heard, he'd once had a church on Gallup Row full of fine gentlemen and generous, charitable ladies. But a love of Congreve's port wine and gambling on racing snails had proved his undoing. The archbishop had dealt with the resulting scandal by sending him to a rundown chapel in the quays. There, he'd kept himself to himself. But when the gangs snapped their fingers, he jumped. The good reverend was clearly nervous – but then who wouldn't be in this gloomy graveyard, surrounded by Gatling Quays' most fearsome inhabitants?

'G-g-good m-m-morning, M-Mr Mc-Mc-Mc-Mc . . .'

With the other pallbearers, Thump laid the coffin gently down beside the grave amongst the wreaths and bouquets already delivered and waiting. Then he slowly straightened up, flexed his shoulders and smiled at the Reverend Spool.

'Mc . . . *Connell*,' said the hapless vicar, spitting the name out at last. His face was so pale, it looked as though the Flour Bag Mob had paid him a recent visit.

'If such a morning as this can be called "good", Vicar,' said Thump, nodding down at the coffin solemnly.

'Ind-d-d-d-d-deed,' stuttered the vicar, his tongue hammering against his teeth like a woodpecker's beak, while his cheeks and ears abruptly turned the same colour as the purple sash that hung down over his priestly robes.

I have to say, given the state of him, I didn't hold up much hope for the service – and I knew that Thump McConnell would not take kindly to the Emperor's sendoff being spoiled by the vicar's inability to string a sentence together. Yet, from the moment he began to recite the burial rites, the Reverend Spool's voice was transformed into one as clear, as deep, and as unbroken as a tolling bell.

'We have come here today, before God,' he intoned, 'to remember our brother and to commit his body . . .'

Above our heads, a raven spiralled down out of the sky, letting out a loud rasping shriek that made the vicar and several of the onlookers jump. It was followed by several more of its noisy brothers. The hoarse, screeching cries grew louder as more and more of the jet-black birds swooped down to the graveyard, their finger-like wing-tips scraping the needles of the yew trees as they came in to land. They perched at the ends of the spreading branches, which bowed under their weight, opened their great ebony-like beaks and screeched so loudly that the vicar had to raise his voice to be heard above the raucous cawing.

There were two dozen of them – a haber-dasher's handful – and as I counted them, it seemed to me as if a thirteenth gang from the quays had arrived to pay its respects. They sat in a circle, their heads cocked and cold black eyes glinting as they watched the pallbearers lower the coffin down into the gaping hole.

'Earth to earth,' the vicar intoned, tossing a handful of claggy mud down on the lid of the coffin. 'Ashes to ashes. Dust to dust.'

Heads bowed, we murmured a final prayer, and then it was over. The circle of mourners broke up, and gang members began to file away. I was about to follow them, when Will tugged the sleeve of my coat.

'What are *they* doing?' he hissed.

I turned and looked back. Gravediggers had appeared, to shovel the mound of earth back into the grave. One of them, however, had climbed down onto the top of the coffin. I heard a soft jangling sound. Meanwhile, the second had thrust a long pole, its top curved like a shepherd's crook, into the ground just to the left of the headstone, and was attaching a bell from the hook. The next moment, the first gravedigger re-emerged and climbed from the grave, a length of chain clasped in his hand.

Ada had done her job well, I noted. I looked round at Will.

'It's an extra that the higher class of undertakers provide,' I told him grimly. 'Insurance against being buried alive.'

I heard Will take a sharp intake of breath. The first gravedigger reached up and attached the gold ring at the end of the chain to the bell. The other end, I knew, was already looped round the Emperor's right index finger. I nodded down into the grave.

'It's just in case the doctor has been a little hasty. If the dear departed wakes up in the coffin, he can pull on the chain, ring the bell, and the graveyard watchmen will dig him up again.'

'Buried alive . . .' Will breathed. 'Can you *imagine?*'

I couldn't, and I didn't want to. But I knew there were many who did. When sickness swept through the city – like the blackwater fever epidemic of a few years ago, or last summer's outbreak of bloody flux – wiping out great swathes of the population, the overworked doctors hadn't always been as scrupulous as they might have been. There had been more than a few stories of those who had been pronounced dead, only to wake up in pitch-black darkness six feet under. That was why those who could afford it paid for a finger-chain and bell to be attached. Some went even further. Theodore Boyle – a millionaire financier – had, on falling ill, changed his will, insisting that he be beheaded after his death and he had employed a samurai swordsman in advance to carry out the deed.

'Come, Will,' I said, clapping my hand on his shoulder. 'Enough of these morbid thoughts. Let's be off.'

The pair of us turned to go. The graveyard had emptied quickly after the burial. The vicar had already gone, as had the funeral carriage, while the last of the mourners were hurrying through the arched entrance. We trudged after them through the wet grass, glancing back nervously over our shoulders as we wound our way between the centuries of graves. The ravens had stopped shrieking, but were still there, their black wings folded round their plump bodies making them look like a group of sinister black cowled monks.

The next moment, as one, the entire flock clapped its wings and flapped up noisily into the air, the raucous cawing louder than ever. Leaving that eerie place, we turned onto the Belvedere Mile and climbed to the rooftop of a tea-importer's warehouse. Through a gap in the buildings behind us, the graveyard was still visible, the thick fog swirling round the dark trees like curdled milk. Above it, the ravens circled.

'That place gives me the collywobbles,' said Will, his voice trembling.

'Don't worry, Will,' I said. 'Old Firejaw's dead and gone, and we've paid our respects, so there's no reason for us ever to go there again.'

Little did I realize, as those fateful words left my lips, just how wrong they would prove to be . . .

CHAPTER 4

A few weeks later – the memory of that bleak funeral having faded from my mind like a night-watchman's brazier at dawn – I dropped in on my old friend, the eminent zoologist Professor Pinkerton-Barnes. I was in a cheerful mood, and with good reason.

My protégé, Will Farmer, had just landed his first highstacking job. An apothecary by the name of Arnold Tilling had taken Will on as his regular tick-tock lad, to deliver potions and pills to his many customers all over town. Now Will was practising his high-stacking skills over the city's rooftops, from noisy Potter's Reach, the air ringing with the tapping and banging of its coopers, wheelwrights and coppersmiths, to hushed Blackchapel with its barristers and clerics; from flea-bitten Eastgate to toffee-nosed Chalfont; from silk emporia in the opulent Asquith Arcade to grubby attics in the rundown Wasps' Nest . . .

I was delighted for him, and with his wages he'd been able to afford to take attic rooms next to mine and invest in a fine new coalstack hat and gamekeeper's waistcoat. Smiling to myself at Will's good fortune, I shinned down a drainpipe to the windowledge of the professor's laboratory and climbed inside.

The professor – or PB to his friends – was perched on a green velvet-upholstered ottoman, a raised scientific journal obscuring his face. I cleared my throat. He jumped, sat upright, and the journal fell to the floor with a soft clatter.

'Barnaby!' he cried out. 'You startled me!'

'Sorry, PB!' I said. 'I—' The words stuck in my throat. 'What have you *done*?'

'Done?' he said.

'Your eyes,' I said, nodding towards the two thick black circular marks that ringed them. 'You look like a panda!'

The professor frowned, took off his spectacles and crossed the room to a large mirror, where he examined his reflection for a moment.

'Oh, I see what you mean,' he said with a chuckle. 'It appears to be residue from the resin I used to seal the goggles . . .'

'Goggles?' I echoed.

'Yes,' said the professor, dabbing at his panda eyes with a grubby handkerchief. 'I was trying to make them watertight – but to no avail. They leaked horribly. Still, I've come up with something much better . . .'

The professor paused when he saw the

puzzled look on my face. Polishing his spectacles on the front of his lab coat before putting them on, he took me by the arm.

'First things first, Barnaby, my boy.' He smiled. 'There's something I want to show you.'

As he ushered me across the laboratory to the marble worktop at the opposite end, I began to detect a distinct smell of rotten fish. He stopped in front of a long, deep metal tray and removed the lid. The smell became eye-wateringly bad.

'Bit of a pong,' the professor conceded, 'but you get used to it.'

I wasn't so sure. With one hand clamped over my nose and mouth, I blinked away the tears and looked down. On the tray lay half a dozen fish, each one a different species. I recognized them all from fishmongers' slabs in the city markets. There was a cod, a mackerel, a sea trout and a herring; a flat plaice, its skin as speckled as the sea-bed sand it had been resting upon, and a long spotted dogfish. Each of them was disfigured by a circular burn-like welt on its body, where the scales were gone and the flesh beneath was blistered and raw.

'I collected them in the harbour,' he said, picking up a pair of long tweezers and prodding the fish. 'All of them were dead and floating on the surface of the water.'

'What do you think happened, PB?' I asked, my voice muffled since I didn't want to remove my hand.

'I'm not sure,' the professor said with a shake of his head. 'But I have a theory . . .' He smiled brightly, his teeth flashing and his two black eyes crinkling up. 'Though I'll need your help, Barnaby.'

I nodded enthusiastically. 'Of course,' I told him. 'Always happy to oblige, you know that.'

Professor Pinkerton-Barnes had theories on everything, from the accents of barking dogs to the kleptomania of magpies; from high-jumping field voles to cat-savaging bullfinches. Most of these theories, I have to concede, proved wrong – but this never dimmed the professor's enthusiasm, and working for him was endlessly fascinating.

'Tonight, I want you to row out into the harbour with me, to explore the base of the harbour rock.'

'The *base*?' I said, intrigued. The harbour rock stood in the middle of the bay between Gatling Quays and the Riverhythe docks, its rocky top festooned with nesting seabirds; its base, twelve fathoms or more under the water. 'But how?'

'You'll see, Barnaby, my boy,' smiled the professor, his panda eyes twinkling, 'tonight.'

And so it was that, as the bell at the top of the East Batavia Trading Company building chimed the three-quarter hour, I found myself down by the lapping water at Riverhythe. It was Sunday night, and apart from a couple of drunken sailors who had been thrown out of taverns and were returning to their ships, and the crew of a night fishing-skiff, the quayside was quiet. I walked along the harbour wall, the stubby Spruton Bill lighthouse to my right, flashing its warnings from the treacherous mudflats as the moon rose. A lone cormorant perched on a jagged rock beside it, wings open and long black neck stretched. Herring gulls wheeled overhead, mewling like babies.

The mooring berths I passed were full of ships, large and small, from grandiose tea clippers to humble barges. Some had travelled from the other side of the world. The coal-driven *Tantalus* from the Moluccas with its cargo of hardwood, for instance; the double-funnelled *Ocean Lord* out of Valparaiso laden with copper-ore, and an elegant junk, the flag of a crimson dragon flapping from the top of its central mast, which had sailed all the way from the East China Sea with its silks, spices and lacquered cabinets.

I continued along the wall to the jetties where the smaller fishing vessels were moored. A light mist danced over the surface of the water and the boards beneath my feet bowed and creaked. To my left and right, the moored boats – their ropes secured to weather-beaten capstans – bobbed about on the low swell.

I nodded greetings to a couple of leathery-faced fishermen who were removing their snapping catch from a mound of gathered lobster-pots. Beyond them, I caught sight of a handful of purple-cheeked fishwives – their hands red raw and aprons splattered with fishy innards – as they gutted and filleted the haddocks and herrings ready for the early-morning markets, and tossed them into waiting baskets.

'Barnaby!' a voice rang out. 'Over here!'

The professor was down on his knees at the very end of the jetty, head raised and waving. I waved back.

'Good evening, PB,' I called, as I approached. 'Not late, I hope.'

'No, no,' he replied cheerfully. 'Punctual as ever. I was just making sure everything was ready.'

Lying on the boards beside the kneeling professor was an unusual-looking boilersuit. It seemed to be made out of oilskin, with gloves and boots seamlessly attached.

'What's this?' I asked.

'This,' said the professor, the pride in his voice unmistakable, 'is what I call a "Neptune" suit. It's made from the finest oiled linen and treated with my own patent mixture of rubber and wax, designed to insulate the wearer and allow ventilation for underwater exploration.'

'I see,' I said quietly.

'Now, instead of goggles and a mouth-piece,' the professor continued, 'I've come up with this.'

He turned to a small wooden crate behind him. I watched as he unclicked the latch and lifted the lid. He reached in with both hands and, with a little grunt of effort, removed a metal helmet, fashioned from bolted sections of brass and inset with a glass panel.

'There!' he announced. 'The "breathing-hood". A trifle heavy and cumbersome, I grant you, but it doesn't leak – and it won't give you panda eyes!'

'You want me to put on this Neptune suit of yours and go for an underwater stroll around the harbour rock?' I asked.

The professor was always full of surprises, but this one took the scullery maid's biscuit.

'That's the general idea, Barnaby, my boy,' said the professor cheerfully. 'And while you're down there, I'd like you to collect some limpets. You see, I have a theory . . .'

I was all ears. The professor employed me because he knew I was adventurous and loved a challenge. Who else would have climbed Sir Rigby Robeson's statue in the middle of Centennial Park to study bullfinches? Or flown a kite from the dome of the Gaiety Theatre in a thunderstorm? But with the Neptune suit, the professor was setting me his sternest challenge yet. Taking off my jacket, waistcoat and shoes, I picked up the oilskin boilersuit and clambered into it, while the professor explained his theory.

The material of the suit was stiff and ungiving, and it creaked when I moved – but it was a good fit. The professor had clearly had me in mind when he made it. Talking excitedly, he climbed into the small rowing boat moored to the jetty, and I followed him, clasping the breathing-hood under one arm.

It turned out that the professor's theory concerned a certain type of exotic mollusc, from the other side of the world, that he believed had been brought into the harbour on the hulls of the incoming cargo ships. The Kuching scorpion limpet is believed to detach itself and hunt fish on the ocean currents, paralysing and feeding off them before returning to its rocky base at night. The professor was convinced that a colony of these shellfish had established itself at the base of the harbour rock and was responsible for the dead fish he'd discovered in the vicinity.

Untying the mooring rope and seizing the oars, the professor proceeded to row us away from the jetty and out into the harbour. He was a thin man, bony and narrow-shouldered – a typical academic – and I was surprised by how expertly he manoeuvred the rowing boat and how vigorously he pulled on the oars. The professor must have noticed, because he told me proudly that he'd rowed for his university as a student. He'd clearly lost little of his skill. We soon left the jetties behind us and, with the professor's strong even strokes, travelled across the harbour and out into the deeper water near the harbour rock.

As we approached, the seabirds nesting in the crevices of the tall crags screeched and took to the air, wheeling in circles overhead. The professor stopped rowing, put down his oars and took the breathing-hood from me. I watched as he carefully clamped the end of a long coil of rubber tubing to a brass fitting on the helmet. The other end was attached to a contraption lying at the professor's feet that resembled a pair of furnace bellows.

'I shall pump breathable air into the hood from the ventilator here,' he explained, placing the helmet on my head.

He tightened a series of wing nuts to the suit's collar, ensuring it was watertight, while I got used to the peculiar sensation of being inside his Neptune suit. The gull-call and lapping water were silenced; the tangy smells of seaweed and salt water were replaced with a metallic odour, laced with something pungent like bitumen or burnt rubber, while my vision was reduced to the little rectangle of the glass panel.

'All right?' the professor asked, his voice sounding muffled and distant.

'I'm fine,' I said, my own words echoing inside the helmet.

'Climb into the water, holding onto the side of the boat,' the professor instructed, as he attached a rope to a buckle on the suit. 'When you let go, the weight of the helmet will take you to the bottom. Just breathe normally, and don't panic.'

I nodded, my breathing sounding incredibly loud inside the helmet.

'When you want to come up, tug on this rope and I'll pull you to the surface. There's a full moon, but it'll still be dark down there, so you'll need these.'

He held up a small axe in one hand and

what looked like a cross between a harpoon and a firework in the other.

'This end is an underwater flare,' the professor explained. 'Pull on the cord and a magnesium compound is released and reacts with the water. It'll give off a bright light for a minute or so, should you need it. Chip off as many limpets as you can. They'll be dormant at this hour and shouldn't give you any trouble.'

I hoped he was right. The professor brought his face up close to the glass panel and grinned toothily.

'All set?' he queried.

'All set,' I replied grimly.

With the professor's help, I climbed up on the bench-board at the rear of the boat, stepped onto the side of the stern and looked down. Out here, beyond the constant swirl of the inner harbour round the wharves, the sea was relatively clear, despite the gathering sea-fret which coiled above it.

The professor tapped me on the shoulder, and I turned and nodded. It was time to take the plunge and, not for the first time, I had to place my trust in the professor and his inventions. He had yet to let me down. I bent forward and stepped backwards, feet first, into the choppy sea.

As I entered the water, I felt a cold pressure grip me firmly from all sides. Taking the harpoon-flare in one hand and the axe in the other, I let go of the side of the boat and began to sink slowly, the heavy helmet weighting me just as the professor had promised it would. Down, down, I went. The water grew darker, but I was still able to see small silver fish darting about me in the pea-green depths. After what seemed like an eternity, but was probably no more than half a minute, my feet came to rest on the soft sandy ground of the sea bed.

Just ahead of me loomed the black silhouette of the harbour rock. I concentrated on steadying my breathing while my ears grew accustomed to the wheezing of the air being pumped into the helmet. The Neptune suit, with its breathing-hood, seemed to be working. I could see my exhaled breath expelled from a side-valve and drifting up to the surface in a string of gleaming bubbles.

With long, loping strides, I crossed the sea bed, clouds of sediment rising up with every footstep. It was dark and gloomy down there, twelve fathoms under, and the currents were strong. I fought my way to within touching-distance of a dark outcrop and, wedging the axe under my left arm, freed my right hand to pull the cord on the underwater flare. There was a fizzling spark, then a sudden flaring flash at the end of the stick, and the surface of the harbour rock was thrown into brilliant relief.

It was then that I saw it . . .

The dark outcrop detached itself from the rock face and unfurled before me. I realized this was no limpet, scorpion or otherwise. In fact, apart from seaweed and green moss, the harbour rock was entirely devoid of life. Instead, staring back at me through hideous pink eyes was the stuff of submarine nightmares, a loathsome sea serpent of appalling size.

Its body alone must have been eight feet long and was as thick as a tea-clipper's mast. It was fringed, top and bottom, with a ruff of mottled spines, while two muscular fins on either side flexed and flicked like draymen's whips. But it was the creature's head that was its most monstrous feature. Inches from the diving helmet, it was blunt and shovel-shaped, the top side pitted and scratched from countless encounters, and those cold deep-set pink eyes embedded on either side of a whiplash barbelled snout.

It raised its head and, through the glass panel of the breathing-hood, I found myself staring down into the sea monster's

Staring back at me was the stuff of submarine nightmares . . .

terrifying maw; a cavernous dark hole surrounded by circle upon concentric circle of hooked, razor-sharp fangs. A tongue unfurled, thick and fibrous and set with three chisel-like teeth, as the creature lunged towards me.

Suddenly, everything was a blur of movement. In my panic I dropped the flare – *and* harpoon – which disappeared on the current. But I managed to grab the axe in my right hand as, with a hideous scraping noise, I felt the creature's sucker-like mouth latch onto my left arm, which I had raised instinctively to protect my head. My screams reverberating around the metal helmet, I hacked blindly at the writhing, flexing body of the monster, even as I felt the corrosive sting of its bite sinking into my forearm through the oilskin.

Repeatedly, I brought the steel axe down, puncturing the creature's black scaly skin, penetrating the rubbery flesh beneath and then wrenching the blade free again. The water around us boiled and frothed with black scales, clumps of white flesh and billowing clouds of red blood.

Then, all at once – as abruptly as it had started – it was over. The creature released its grip on my arm and I tumbled backwards, the strong harbour current sweeping me from my feet and carrying me off, away from the harbour rock. Too late, as I was swept away, I realized that in my frenzy I had severed the rope that tethered me to the professor's boat. At the same moment, a tremendous jerking wrench at my neck told me that the breathing tube had reached the end of its extent.

There sounded, by my right ear, a *pop* like a cork flying from a champagne bottle. The tube had broken free of the valve on the helmet and the breathing-hood suddenly began to fill with water.

I gulped in a last mouthful of air and

then struck out for the surface, fighting the weight of the brass helmet – a moment earlier, the means of survival; now the cause of peril. Those moments in the dark waters of the harbour, being swept away on a current and fighting to get to the surface, were the longest of my life and, as the salt water rose in the helmet, filling my ears and stinging my eyes, I truly believed that they were to be my last.

Then, after a seeming lifetime of flailing, kicking, spluttering effort, my feet connected with a deep shelf of shingle. I clawed my way up it in a rattling avalanche of pebbles, the heavy helmet pressing down on my shoulders and my head ready to explode.

All at once, the helmet burst through the surface of the water and I found myself peering through the fogged glass at the shore. Dragging my exhausted body the last few yards, I made it up out of the shallows and collapsed in a heap on the mud, water draining out of the helmet like ale from an upturned –

'The Gatling Sump,' I whispered. 'Of all places . . .'

Just beyond the sewer-opening was a place I thought I'd never have to set foot in again. Now, I realized, I had little choice. The graveyard lay between me and the jetty at Riverhythe – towards which, no doubt, a shocked and distraught professor was rowing with all his might.

I could have taken the long way round, back towards the Belvedere Mile and through the warehouses of Gatling Quays, but I was a tick-tock lad – wet, bedraggled and half-drowned, but a tick-tock lad none-theless. I didn't take the long way round. I took short cuts, and the shortest cut of all was through Adelaide Graveyard.

I made my way along the black railings, went through the cemetery gates and was striding between the dark silent grave-stones, when a sound made me stop in my tracks.

It was the sound of a tinkling bell . . .

CHAPTER 5

*T*here it was again, faint but unmistakable. Somewhere in Adelaide Graveyard, a finger-chain was ringing a headstone bell. I stopped and peered about me at the eerie array of gravestones, tomb slabs and memorial statuary that stretched away into the mist.

The bell sounded again.

Perhaps some nocturnal animal – a wharf rat or feral cat – had become entangled in the chain and was simply struggling to break free. The alternative was too horrible to contemplate.

I stumbled on through the graveyard, scanning the headstones around me as I went,

hoping desperately that I was right and that this was a false alarm. A new burial with a finger-chain and bell was meant to be watched over for anything up to six days, depending on the fee. As the bell continued to ring, I fully expected a licensed gravewatcher, spade in hand, to emerge from the sentry box I was rapidly approaching through the mist. But when I got there, the box was deserted, and the brazier in front of it unlit and stone-cold.

Looking up, I glimpsed the tall tenement building of Adelaide Mansions overlooking the far side of the graveyard. A single square of light on the left of its dark façade showed that Ada Gussage's rooms were the only ones still occupied.

I shivered violently, and winced as the dull ache in my left arm became more insistent. A wave of nausea washed over me and I crouched, head between my knees, to wait for it to pass. Blood was thumping in my head and I felt suddenly hot and feverish – but the feeling of sickness passed.

Straightening up, my Neptune suit creaking like a carriage horse's harness, I continued on through Adelaide Graveyard. Out of the swirling mist, the stony-eyed angels on the grander tombs and gravestones stared down at me impassively, their spreading wings strangely menacing in the moonlight.

I felt light-headed and dizzy, but the intense darts of pain which now shot up my arm jolted me back to reality. I had to get to Riverhythe.

The bell sounded again, close now, and as it did so, I stumbled and lost my balance, pitching forward onto a wet, grassy mound, the diving helmet tumbling from my grasp. I twisted round, groaning as the pain in my injured arm flared like a phosphorus match, to find my feet entangled in a funeral wreath, its splendid blooms withered to a tangle of twigs and blackened flower heads. A sodden ribbon trailed across the grass, gold letters on crimson – *To our beloved boss. Gone but not forgotten. The Sumpside Boys.* The words shimmered in front of my eyes and my head began to swim.

With a low moan, I sank back, another wave of nausea breaking over me. The frosty dew-filled grass felt wonderfully cool and, as I pressed my feverish face against it, I began to feel a little better.

Just then, the bell sounded directly above me.

Turning my head to the side, I opened one eye. Silvery moonlight glinted on a crook-like pole, a taut metal chain and, at its end, a small copper bell hesitantly swinging to and fro. I looked up. The inscrutable eyes of the stone angel at the top of the gravestone stared down at me. Beams of moonlight crossed the shiny black granite surface, momentarily picking out the letters engraved upon it.

EDWIN "FIREJAW" O'ROURKE, I read.

"Cruelly taken from this World in his 52nd year.
A mighty red-maned lion amongst men,
The Quays shall not see his like again."

The bell suddenly stopped ringing, and with it, my heart seemed to skip a beat. There was no animal caught in the finger-chain. It ran unbroken from the headstone bell down into the ground, some six feet or more, to the metal ring on Firejaw O'Rourke's dead finger . . .

I lay there, paralysed with fear, my feverish head pressed into the cool dew-soaked grass. And then I heard it, almost imperceptible at first, the faintest of faint scratching.

As I listened, the scratching grew louder, turning to a hideous scraping, clawing sound. Suddenly, beneath me, the ground began to tremble. With a raw, choking cry of terror, I threw myself back as the grassy turf erupted, inches from where my head had been.

A massive clenched hand – every nail and

knuckle embedded with mud – burst up from the ground, followed closely by a second, sending a hail of mud and earth high in the air. As I watched, transfixed by the horror of the scene, the grave before me burst open, clods of earth, splintered coffin wood and blackened funeral wreaths flying in all directions.

A great dark shape heaved itself out of the debris and rose to its feet like some wilderness bear roused from hibernation. It stood with its back to me, head bowed towards the marble headstone, as if reading the epitaph.

Trembling uncontrollably, I began to back away on hands and knees, the Neptune suit creaking and squeaking with every movement. The dark, silver-tinged clouds overhead parted, and the graveyard was bathed in moonlight. Slowly, Firejaw O'Rourke turned to face me.

The Emperor's fine funeral clothes – embroidered jacket and intricately pleated cravat;

Slowly, Firejaw O'Rourke turned to face me.

black-and-white checked breeches with the padded yellow cummerbund tight around a great sagging gut – were crumpled and smeared in dark mud. A gold ring glistened on the index finger of one massive hand, the finger-chain now ripped free, and a sickly-sweet cloying smell filled the air that was the unmistakable odour of rotting flesh.

But it wasn't these details that seared themselves into my memory so that even now, when I think of it, I break out in a cold sweat. No, it was the sight that greeted me when Firejaw O'Rourke turned his face towards mine.

On those ghastly features, etched into the decaying flesh, was the awful history of the Emperor of Gatling Quays' death; a boatload of exploding fireworks and the murky waters of the harbour. Burned and drowned, Firejaw stared down at me through one white, sightless eye. The left-hand side of his face was bloodless, with mottled blue blotches and a greenish hue to the lips and cheek. His great beard, flecked with mud, blazed a reddish ginger, made even more vivid by the colourless features above.

On the right side of his face, the red beard had been burned away and the skin hung down his cheek and neck in looped waxen ribbons, clinkers and ashes embedded in the formless mass. The lips were blistered and fused together on one side. The right ear had melted completely and, with the molten skin now set without it, it was impossible to see where once it had been. As for the nose, the left-hand side was intact, but the right half had been eaten away by flames to reveal the dark cavity beneath, bone-edged and blackened.

As the Emperor of Gatling Quays towered over me, the mist seemed to thicken, along with the insistent thumping of blood in my temples and the searing pain shooting up my arm. I fell back and shut my eyes, willing the nightmare to end. The stench of rotting flesh grew stronger. Pebbles and earth peppered me as silken coat-tails brushed past my cheek, accompanied by heavy ponderous footfalls and a soft squelching sound, like overripe fruit being crushed underfoot.

When I opened my eyes, I was lying in front of an empty grave, strewn with funereal wreckage. The stone angel – wings spread wide – gazed down at me through the mist and, in my feverish half-crazed state, I thought I saw a shudder pass through its body and ruffle its feathers.

That was enough for me. Grasping the professor's precious breathing-hood, I clambered to my feet and blundered through the graveyard, towards the glowing streetlamps by the entrance gate in the distance – and escape.

My head was swimming. What had I just seen? Firejaw O'Rourke had been dead and buried two weeks earlier, and yet hadn't I just witnessed the Emperor of Gatling Quays digging himself out of his own grave?

I had read of such things happening in the distant islands of the Indies in *Crockford's Journal of the Unnatural* during my studies at Underhill's Library for Scholars of the Arcane. But here, in the city, in Gatling Quays ... ?

My mind racing, I reached a pool of yellow light at the graveyard gate, only to feel a hand on my shoulder. With a yelp of terror, I pulled free, the diving helmet raised above my head ready to smash down into Firejaw O'Rourke's hideous face.

'Lawks-a-mussy!' exclaimed Ada Gussage, pulling her dark woollen shawl round her heavy shoulders and pushing her big red face into mine. 'You look as though you've seen a ghost ...'

CHAPTER
6

*A*da Gussage's face hovered before me, her currant-bun eyes glinting with concern.

'I'm sorry if I startled you, Barnaby Grimes!' she exclaimed. 'But I thought I saw figures moving about down here in the graveyard. Spooks and ghouls my neighbours would have said – but Ada Gussage doesn't believe in such tomfoolery. No, I was thinking it was graverobbers more like, out to dig up poor folk's bodies to sell to those anatomizers and surgeon butchers in Hartley Square and the like.'

I swallowed hard, my tongue so dry it felt

as though it was glued to the top of my mouth. I was sweating and shivering, and my temples throbbed.

'Adelaide Graveyard wouldn't be the first those bone merchants have disturbed just lately,' she whispered conspiratorially. 'And it won't be the last, you mark my words, Barnaby Grimes.' She raised her eyebrows. 'Here, I don't suppose you've spotted a certain gentleman hanging around, have you? Wears a long black cape trimmed with ocelot fur and a swanky high hat with a dark-red band. He's one of them graverobbers, I'd bet my last brass farthing on it . . .'

I shook my head weakly, trying hard to concentrate on her words and banish the nightmarish vision of the Emperor from my thoughts.

'Pity,' she said. 'I bet he's a doctor or some such,' she went on, her sing-song voice ringing in my head. 'Now, a nice cup of tea, that's what you need, Barnaby Grimes. A cup of smoked Assam to keep the cold out.'

'Tea,' I murmured. 'Tea.'

'That's right, a cup of tea,' she smiled. 'You come back with me, young Barnaby. Ada Gussage'll see you right . . .'

'No, no,' I said. 'Thank you, Ada, but I'm in a hurry. I've got to get to Riverhythe. That's why I took a short cut through the graveyard and—'

'And what, Barnaby?' she said, her face looming closer. 'What did you see?'

'I don't have time now,' I muttered as Firejaw O'Rourke's hideous face sprang into my mind. 'The professor . . . he'll be worried. Waiting . . . must get back to him . . .'

I turned and staggered away, the breathing-hood clamped under my arm. Behind me I heard Ada Gussage firing off questions. Was I all right? Why was I dressed in those funny clothes? Could she help in any way? I had no energy to respond. I needed all my reserves to make it to Riverhythe. She called after me, telling me to 'watch my step' and 'take care', before – as I turned a corner – her voice faded away.

There was no question of my returning to the short cut through the Adelaide Graveyard. Instead, I resigned myself to taking the long way round to the jetties at Riverhythe, along the harbour wall.

The harbourside was all but deserted. As I stumbled on, my head pounding and my legs like lead weights, it was all I could do to put one foot in front of the other. The fog-blurred moon was low in the sky, spotting the tops of the waves with muted silver and casting shadows across the cobbled harbour wall. With so few people out and about, embold-ened rats had emerged from their filthy holes. They scurried this way and that, snatching any food they could find – cabbage leaves and onion skins; spilt grain . . . Half a dozen of them squabbled over a rotting pumpkin, gorging themselves on the orange pulp, oblivious to my presence as I staggered past them.

A deep sonorous sound echoed across the harbour, and I looked up to see the Spruton Bill lighthouse flashing from the mudflats in the distance. The foghorn sounded again as I approached the jetties of Riverhythe.

'Barnaby!' a familiar voice rang out. 'Barnaby, my boy.'

It was the professor. His coat was open and his hair was flapping wildly as he came running along one of the jetties, his footsteps hammering on the wooden boards.

'Oh, my word, Barnaby,' he cried out, his voice high and tremulous, 'how glad I am to see you. I was about to call the Harbour Constabulary and get them to trawl the harbour.' He shook his head. 'My theory about the Kuching scorpion limpets was quite wrong. You'll never guess what I found—' He fell still, his look of relief giving way to one of concern. 'But, my dear boy!

You're injured! Let me take a look . . .'

As the professor took my arm, a pain of such intensity shot through me that I let out an anguished cry. Suddenly, what strength I still had deserted me, my knees buckled and everything went black.

The next thing I knew I was lying on something soft and comfortable. A bright light was shining, turning everything behind my closed eyelids a deep orange-red. For a moment I lay there, listening to the sound of a bird chirping close by, and the soft clatter of wooden spoons in metal pots in the background.

I opened my eyes and looked round. Fluffy white clouds were flitting across the sky outside the window; a pert sparrow was perched on the ledge.

'Ah, Barnaby,' the professor called across the room. 'You're awake!'

Sitting up on one elbow, I watched as he

poured a pale green liquid from a saucepan into a mug and then hurried across the laboratory to the makeshift bed – an upholstered sofa, strewn with blankets – where I lay. He held out the steaming beverage, and my nostrils quivered at the spicy aroma.

'Madderwort tisane,' he said. 'Wonderful restorative qualities.'

'So, how long have I been asleep exactly?' I asked, as I raised the sweet-smelling drink to my lips and took a small sip.

The professor seized the fob-watch which hung from a chain at the front of his high-buttoned waistcoat, and examined it. He frowned, and I watched his lips move as he performed a quick calculation.

'Thirty-seven hours,' he said.

'Thirty-seven hours!' I spluttered, madderwort tisane joining the other stains down the front of PB's grubby lab coat. 'But . . . but that makes it . . .'

'Tuesday,' said the professor. 'Tuesday

afternoon. One thirty-seven, to be precise.' He returned the watch to his waistcoat pocket and tutted sympathetically. 'You've been very poorly, Barnaby, my boy.'

'Poorly!' I exclaimed, putting the mug aside and jumping to my feet. 'But . . . why didn't you wake me, PB? I've got business to attend to . . .'

Suddenly, I felt extremely groggy. My head swam and all the strength seemed to go out of my legs. I sat back down heavily on the sofa and held my head in my hands.

Tuesday already! But what about all my *Monday* appointments? A tick-tock lad's reputation was built on punctuality. In my line of work, I couldn't afford to be late.

'I've been carrying out experiments,' said the professor. 'The creature that attacked you appears to have had a poisonous bite. A slow-acting venom, by my calculations. Quite fascinating!' He nodded towards the window, where an oilskin boilersuit was draped over the back of a chair. 'If it hadn't been for the Neptune suit, it could have been a whole lot worse . . .'

Slowly, everything started to come back to me. I'd been on a diving expedition, and been attacked underwater . . .

'I dressed the wound,' the professor was saying, leaning forward and touching the bandage on my arm gently, 'with a sphagnum-moss poultice to draw the poison.' He smiled. 'The Inupiaq people of the Arctic swear by it.'

'But what *was* it?' I asked. 'The creature that attacked me?'

'Come, I'll show you,' said the professor.

I started back with surprise. 'You have it here?' I said.

The professor nodded. 'I fished it out of the harbour,' he said. 'You did a very good job of finishing it off, Barnaby. Mind you,' he added, chuckling softly, 'it wasn't easy getting it back here – particularly since I also had an unconscious tick-tock lad to contend with.'

This time, I climbed to my feet more slowly. I paused for a moment to wait for the room to stop spinning.

'It's called a black-scaled lamprey,' the professor explained as he helped me across the laboratory. 'They're usually found in the tropical waters of the East.'

He led me to an imposing glass tank at the far end of the laboratory, where the dead creature hung suspended in a solution of pale yellow formaldehyde. I took a sharp intake of breath. Even in death, the lamprey was a formidable sight.

'This fine specimen probably reached our shores by gripping the hull of a cargo ship with those impressive jaws,' the professor explained. 'Its bite is remarkably strong – and, as I say, ferociously venomous.' He smiled sheepishly. 'But then I don't have to tell you that, do I, Barnaby?'

I shook my head grimly, staring once more at those circles of savage hooked teeth that ringed its dark gullet; teeth that had embedded themselves so painfully in my arm. I could also see the savage marks left on the creature's grotesque head and neck where I'd repeatedly driven home the blade of the axe in my frenzied efforts to escape.

Suddenly, the extraordinary events of that terrifying night came tumbling back to me in a rush. The sea monster, the near drowning – and the hideous apparition I'd seen in the graveyard . . .

'PB,' I began, 'something else happened that night . . .' And I told the professor all about the gruesome events in the Adelaide Graveyard.

He listened with a thoughtful expression on his face until I was finished. Then, refreshing my cup with more of the herbal infusion, he patted me on the shoulder.

'From what you've told me,' he said, 'I

suspect that the lamprey's venom contains a hallucinogen . . .'

'Hallucinogen?' I queried.

'A mind-altering substance,' the professor explained, 'which quite likely made you see things, Barnaby, that weren't real—'

'You mean I dreamed the whole thing up?' I interrupted incredulously.

'Quite possibly, my boy. Quite possibly.' The professor smiled. 'After all, corpses don't just come to life and dig themselves up, now, do they?'

I had to agree and, although my arm was in a sling and I still felt light-headed, I have to admit I felt a wave of relief wash over me at the thought that Firejaw O'Rourke had not in fact risen from the grave, and that the whole thing had been a hallucination. The professor assured me that the effects of the lamprey's venom had had ample time to wear off, and that I could dispense with the sling in a day or so. He also apologized fervently for unwittingly placing me in such danger – though seemed extremely pleased at how well his precious Neptune suit had performed.

He handed me an envelope as I gathered my things together and prepared to take my leave. It contained twice my normal fee.

'As long as you think you're up to it, Barnaby,' said the professor, patting me on the shoulder as he guided me back across the laboratory. 'Perhaps today, though, you might want to leave by the door rather than the window.'

I laughed. It was sound advice which, for once, I decided to heed. You need two arms, not to mention a clear head, to highstack across the city, and the bite from that scaly lamprey had taken it out of me. Having promised to return later in the week, I bade farewell to the professor and set off.

It felt odd being down on the ground with all the other cobblestone-creepers – and, although not as demanding as highstacking over the rooftops, the streets held more than their own fair share of challenges. For a start, there were the carts and carriages, their whip-wielding drivers hammering along the narrow thoroughfares oblivious to those on foot. Then there were the jostling crowds thronging the narrow pavements; all elbows, shoulder barges and shoves in the back. With my arm in a sling and my head yet to fully clear, I found my walk back to my rooms in Caged Lark Lane every bit as exhausting as a cross-town highstack.

Surfaced with a mix of sea-coal cinders and crushed oyster shells, and lit by a single oil lamppost, Caged Lark Lane was a small alley, just up from the crossroads where Laystall Street crosses Hog Hill – although the casual passer-by could be forgiven for missing it. But then, that's what I liked about Caged Lark Lane. It was a forgotten, overlooked corner of the great teeming city and, apart from J. Bradley-Arnold's paper merchants on the corner and Fettle's Yard, where Hackney carriages were repaired, my apartment house was the only other building in the lane.

Number 3, Caged Lark Lane was old, run-down and in need of repair. Not that I'm complaining. For what they were, my rooms were very reasonable. More importantly, the high roof atop the five-storey building offered both excellent views and easy access to the surrounding rooftops to any highstacker worth his salt.

Today, though, I wouldn't be shinning down the drainpipe and entering through my attic window. Instead, like more conventional occupants, I climbed the stairs to the front door.

As I did so, I heard the words of the neighbourhood newspaper-seller floating through the air. With his wooden leg and eye-patch, Blindside Bailey was an old war veteran supplementing his meagre pension as best he

Blindside Bailey was an old war veteran.

could. By day, he would sell the editions of the newspapers; by night he would entertain the locals in the Goose and Gullet by recounting his past campaigns to any who would stand him a drink. Many's the time I had whiled away an evening, listening to Blindside's tales of a soldier's life in the far-off lands of the East.

'Read all about it!' Blindside Bailey's gruff voice rang out. 'Body of gangland boss taken! Read all about it! Graverobbers ransack gangland leader's grave! Read all about it!'

Turning on my heels, I hurried back to the corner. I exchanged a copper penny for the latest edition of the *Daily Chronicle*, and a cold chill spread down my spine as I started to read.

> 'Yesterday evening, as the good folk of the city slept in their beds, the body of infamous gang leader, Edwin "Firejaw" O'Rourke, was stolen from his final resting place

in Adelaide Graveyard in the Gatling Quays district. Harbourside police suspect grave-robbers, or "resurrection men" as they are known locally, of perpetrating this outrage . . .'

CHAPTER 7

*B*ack in my attic rooms, I collapsed into my old armchair and studied the *Daily Chronicle*. I must admit, my hands were shaking as I scanned the column of small print. It seemed that Firejaw O'Rourke was merely the latest victim of a spate of outrages in cemeteries and graveyards all over town. Ada Gussage had said as much when I ran into her in Adelaide Graveyard, though I had been too spooked and full of lamprey venom to take it in. Now, here it was in front of me in black and white.

The *Chronicle* was of the firm belief that this was the work of graverobbers, or resurrection men – a bunch of individuals so reviled and disreputable that not even the denizens of Gatling Quays would admit to having anything to do with them. Apparently, the corpses they stole ended up on marble slabs in underground dissecting theatres, where students of anatomy would pay handsomely to study them.

You could make a pretty penny from a recently buried corpse. The fresher the body, the higher the price the unscrupulous surgeon would be prepared to pay, no questions asked – and all in the interests of scientific enquiry, of course.

The account in the *Daily Chronicle*, so measured and plausible, seemed to confirm the professor's theory, and I wanted to believe that the ghastly apparition I'd seen in the graveyard was indeed a figment of my imagination brought to vivid life by the venom of an exotic sea creature. Perhaps all I'd really seen was an empty grave, ransacked by graverobbers. The rest was simply a terrible hallucination, just as he had said. Yes, I really did want to believe him – yet it had all seemed so real that doubt still gnawed at the back of my mind . . .

Just then, there came a light *tap-tap* at the window and I looked up to see Will Farmer peering through the grimy glass. I beckoned for him to come in. He pushed the window open and dropped down lightly to the floor.

'Barnaby, where have you been?' he said. 'I was beginning to—' His gaze fell on the sling and a look of concern crossed his face. 'What happened?'

'Pull up a chair, Will,' I said, 'it's a long story.' I shook my head. 'A story which I'm still trying to get straight in my own mind. Some of it is pretty hard to believe . . .'

'Try me,' he said.

And so I recounted the strange events that had taken place over the previous couple of days. Will listened attentively, his eyes growing wider and wider as I described my trip out into the harbour and the underwater battle with the black-scaled lamprey. And when I got to the incident in the graveyard, he jumped back so violently I thought he was going to tumble from his chair.

'Unbelievable,' he gasped.

'I know, Will, I know,' I said. 'The professor says the poison from the lamprey's bite affected my mind, made me see things.'

'So Firejaw O'Rourke didn't rise from the grave?' asked Will, his voice little more than a whisper.

'That's what I keep telling myself,' I said. 'It was so real, and yet . . .' I shook my head. The nagging doubts remained. 'He *can't* be alive, can he, Will? The pair of us saw him being buried two weeks ago.' I looked down and tapped the newspaper folded on my lap. 'Now I read that, according to the *Daily Chronicle*, O'Rourke was dug up by a gang of grave-robbers and his corpse sold for dissection.'

'Dissection?' Will repeated quietly. He frowned. 'Sunday night you were in the graveyard, right?'

I nodded.

'Well, that's interesting,' he said, 'because I noticed something odd on Monday morning. In the early hours, it was.'

'Go on,' I said, leaning forward in my armchair.

'I'd had a dawn drop to do for Mr Tilling the apothecary,' Will went on. 'There'd been an outbreak of damp-lung at St Jude's Hospital and I had an emergency consignment of sulphur and morphia pillules to deliver. Old Mr Tilling had been working all through the night to complete them . . . Anyway, it's half-four when I arrive at the hospital, and still pitch-black. Just as I get there, I see this old wagon pull up, and these two rough-looking types jump down and drag out a long wooden crate . . .'

'A coffin?' I asked.

'Same size,' said Will, 'but not the same shape. Just a long box, really.'

I nodded. 'And what did they do with it?'

'Well, that's the thing,' said Will. 'Instead of going in through the front entrance, they took it round the back, where Bentham was waiting for them.'

'Bentham?' I said.

'The morgue attendant,' said Will, his top lip curling. 'Bulgy eyes and warty skin. None of the nurses can stand him . . . He's a slippery character at the best of times, but he was looking more furtive than ever that morning. Kept glancing round, and I was sure he gave money to the men . . .' Will looked up at me. 'I didn't give it much thought at the time, Barnaby, but it could well have been a body.'

'Firejaw O'Rourke, perhaps?' I asked him.

'I don't know,' said Will. 'The crate was big enough. And after all, it did arrive the morning after his body went missing . . .'

I nodded as a shiver ran down my spine. So

what exactly *had* I witnessed in Adelaide Graveyard in my feverish state? Was it a mere figment of my imagination, or not? I certainly hoped it was. The alternative, that Firejaw O'Rourke had indeed come back to life, was too gruesome to consider. Today was Tuesday. Even if the body had been bound for the dissection table, they couldn't have finished with it already.

'Come on, Will,' I said, climbing to my feet. 'I'm not going to be happy until I've found out one way or the other.'

'The hospital?' he said.

'The hospital.'

With my arm still bundled up in its sling, highstacking was out of the question. Instead, Will and I made our way across town down with all the other cobblestone-creepers. It was late afternoon by now, and the streets were thronging.

We dog-legged through the Laynes – ancient

cobbled alleys lined with tiny workshops that, each day, burst out of their cramped premises onto the street to display their wares. An elbowing crowd jostled one another as bargain-hunters picked their way through stacks and racks of produce, noisily haggling.

I squeezed past a portly dowager, her nose the colour of port-wine and her fleshy arms buried deep in a pile of tawdry lace antimacassars, who was stridently arguing over their price. A rickets-bowed gardener was inspecting a row of spades outside Guthrie's Ironmongery next door. Further on, two grubby children were teasing a small bony dog with the toffee-apple they were sharing, making it leap up, before hiding the sweetmeat behind their backs – and leaving the dog yapping with frustration . . .

As we reached the corner of Marchant Lane and Croup End, the rank odour of the Tivoli Slaughterhouse curdled with the sharp eye-watering tang from Selsey's vinegar factory, filling the air with an unspeakable odour. Covering our noses, we entered Margolies Street, where a mist of pink and white dust filled the air. Sills, steps, kerbs, ledges; every surface in the narrow street was covered in a fine layer of powder.

Four shops along, the curved sign above a pair of wrought-iron gates announced in gothic lettering, *Algernon Mortimer & Company - Monumental Masons*. I peered inside as we passed.

Two stocky men in overalls stood at the centre of a yard, their bodies swathed in the billowing dust as they sawed at a large slab of veined stone. A third man – a red-and-black spotted kerchief tied round his head – was seated on a low stool to their right, chisel and mallet in hand, chipping away at an arch-shaped gravestone. He was whistling something bright and tuneful which rose up above the grinding noise of the stone-cutting, the perky melody at odds with the sombre nature of his job.

Stacked about him in rows were finished headstones, each one awaiting their inscriptions. Black, white, pink and grey; some were extravagant, some modest. There were arched slabs and corniced oblongs. One was carved like a scroll, another like a book, its pages fixed for ever half-open, while several were simple yet elegant crosses made of granite or sandstone.

But it wasn't the gravestones that made me stop and stare, open-mouthed, through the gates of the monumental mason's. No, it was the sight of the carved figures perched above them – stone angels, wings spread wide, hands clasped and heads bowed, their sightless eyes staring down. I shivered uncontrollably as, for a fleeting moment, I was transported back to the horror of Adelaide Graveyard.

I felt a tug on my arm. 'You all right, Barnaby?' Will asked. 'You look as if you've seen a—'

'Don't say it,' I interrupted him. 'Come on, St Jude's is just up ahead.'

We rounded the corner of Bishops Walk and there it was, the tall imposing neo-classical frontage of St Jude's Hospital.

Thirty years earlier, the place had been a scandal – little more than a fever pit from which patients were lucky to get out alive. Its doctors had been the worst kind of sawbones; its nurses gin-soaked drabs. But that had all changed during the last war, when a new kind of nurse had emerged from the army hospitals of the East. These angels of mercy had reformed the appalling conditions in which wounded soldiers had languished, and brought their new methods of sober cleanliness and meticulous order with them when they returned from the war. Now, St Jude's was a model hospital, bringing relief and comfort to the city's sick.

'Busy as ever,' Will commented, as we approached the forbidding entrance.

I nodded. The forecourt was teeming, with numerous horse-drawn carriages jostling for position at the foot of the circular entrance steps, and a constant stream of people going in and coming out of the great studded doors. Some were on crutches, some were on stretchers and, as we climbed the steps, I found myself making diagnoses of the people we passed.

A young child – his face grazed and legs mashed – who was being carried in by his father must have been the victim of a traffic accident. A woman with a gashed arm, the unfortunate target of a rabid dog. While a grey-skinned, sunken-cheeked old man, coughing violently behind a blood-flecked rag as he lay on a wooden stretcher, was clearly consumptive . . .

As Will and I entered the great entrance hall, the atmosphere changed. It was light, warm and pungent. The sooty smell of the lamps which were fixed to the walls mixed with the unmistakable odour of carbolic soap. Nurses in crisp white aprons formed the shuffling patients into orderly lines in the great vaulted hall, and sent them off to various parts of the hospital to have their ailments tended to.

'Broken bones, that way,' snapped a tall nurse in wire-framed spectacles, eyeing my sling and pointing me down a long corridor to the right.

'It's all right, sister,' said Will, stepping in. 'He's with me. We're making a delivery.'

'Oh, afternoon, Will,' said the nurse with a smile. 'Didn't see you there.' She raised her eyes to the vaulted ceiling. 'Chaos it is, today. Absolute chaos . . . No, madam,' she cried out, darting off in pursuit of a portly individual whose face was covered in a suppurating rash. 'I've already told you, the sulphur baths are that way . . .'

We left her to it. Will steered me across the great hall, the floor tiled with pale grey and green marble slabs and inlaid with a wonderful mosaic depicting the Rod of Asclepius; a single green snake, its venomous mouth agape, wrapped around its knotted length.

'The morgue's downstairs,' he told me as we reached the top of a stairwell on the far side.

There were classical scenes painted on the walls of the stairwell: fluttering winged babies dangling grapes before the mouths of voluptuous maidens; centaurs and satyrs, and groups of men with long robes and thick beards. One individual stood out. Taller than the rest, he had a quill in one hand and an axe in the other and, from the top of his head, a small flame burned at the centre of his halo. Will nodded towards him as we headed down the stairs.

'St Jude, himself,' he said.

As we went down the stairs, the sounds from the entrance hall faded. A couple of nurses in crisp white uniforms clutching glowing lanterns passed us, heading in the opposite direction, followed a little later by a doctor, with what I took to be one of those new-fangled wooden stethoscopes tucked into the brim of his top hat. We continued down into the gloomy depths of the great hospital.

At the bottom of the stairs, Will pushed open a pair of dark varnished doors and we entered a large vaulted chamber with rows of wooden trestles stretching away into the shadows. High above our heads a simple chandelier comprising four white candles – three of them burning – hung down from a chain in the centre of the vault.

'Can I 'elp you?' A low cracked voice sounded from behind us.

Turning, I saw a small stooped individual in a grubby apron and black, greased-down hair leering back at us. Tipping me the wink, Will stepped forward and produced a glass vial from his pocket.

'Actually, I think you can,' said Will. 'I'm looking for Dr Fitzroy. I've got the medicine he requested . . .' Will began.

'Medicine?' the man repeated, surprised. 'Don't you know where you are, son? This is the morgue.' He nodded towards the shroud-covered trestles. 'Bit late in the day for medicine for this lot,' he added and croaked with amusement.

'Oh, dear, how stupid of me,' said Will, his voice bright and naive. 'I don't suppose you could . . . ?' His words trailed away.

The morgue attendant tutted and shook his head from side to side. 'I don't know,' he muttered. 'You tick-tock lads! You'd best come with me, son. I'll see you right.'

He took Will by the arm and the pair of them disappeared through the doors, leaving me alone in the morgue. I turned and approached the rows of trestle tables. Every one was covered with a white shroud from beneath which pairs of feet protruded, each with a tag carefully tied to the big toe. I glanced at the first one.

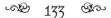

Eliza Morris, I read, the words written in a slanting black copperplate script. *Cause of death: the croup.* And underneath, in bold red capitals: *FOR BURIAL.*

Then at the next, *Thomas Rideout. Cause of death: Heart Failure. FOR BURIAL.*

I continued down the line. *Blow to the head. Apoplexy. Fever . . . FOR BURIAL, FOR BURIAL, FOR BURIAL . . .* Eight trestles along, I paused, my heart hammering in my chest as I read the tag:

Unknown indigent. Cause of death: Drowning. FOR DISSECTION.

The body beneath the shroud was considerably larger than the others. At the head of the table, a wisp of hair was just visible which, in the candlelight, seemed to me to have a hint of ginger about it. My hands were shaking as I leaned forwards. I was hot and cold at the same time. I touched the shroud. As I did so, there was a slight, yet unmistakable, movement from beneath the material. I froze, transfixed.

With a soft thump, an arm slipped off the side of the trestle table and dangled loosely, the fingers of the hand gnarled and twisted. My breath came in sharp gasps. Could this be the graverobbed body of Firejaw O'Rourke?

I had to find out.

Moving up to the top end of the table, I took hold of the material, slowly lifted the white sheet – and let out a cry. It wasn't the Emperor of Gatling Quays at all, but an unfortunate old man at least twenty years his senior, bloated and mottled by harbour water. A tavern drunk most likely, I thought, who'd stumbled on the shoreside cobbles in the dead of night, and whose body had gone unclaimed. The morgue attendant had probably got an arrangement with the Harbour Constabulary – who fished bodies out of the water – and stood to make a few shillings from the doctors upstairs.

But this wasn't the work of graverobbers.

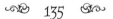

By all accounts, graverobbers dealt in fresh bodies, where there was real money to be made . . . I turned away and checked the rest of the tags. Finding no others for dissection, I headed for the door with a strange mixture of relief and disappointment.

As I pushed open the dark varnished door, I heard a high-pitched scream and found myself face to face with a dazzlingly pretty nurse.

'You startled me!' she gasped, before stooping to pick up the bundle of blank mortuary tags she had been carrying and which now lay scattered at her feet. 'This place always gives me the shivers,' she continued, blushing daintily as I bent to help her. She looked up at me, and frowned. 'You're not Bentham!' she exclaimed.

'I'm afraid I'm lost,' I said. 'Took a wrong turning.' I shrugged, indicating my sling.

She smiled as she gathered the last of the tags and stepped past me to place them on the mortuary attendant's desk beside the door.

Turning quickly away, she pointed to my arm.

'Would you like me to take a look at that arm of yours?' she asked.

'If you wouldn't mind,' I said, smiling back. 'Miss . . . ?'

'My name's Lucy,' she said. 'Lucy Partleby.'

We climbed the stairs, side by side, her with her lamp raised and me stealing glances. She had auburn hair, tied up and crowned with a starched white cap; milky skin, with freckles at the tops of her cheeks and in a line across the bridge of her nose, and the greenest eyes I'd ever seen. She led me down a long tiled corridor to an empty surgery, where she sat me down and began to undo my bandages.

'I must say, this has been dressed very well,' she commented.

'It was my friend who did it,' I told her proudly. 'Professor Pinkerton-Barnes.'

'Quite excellent,' she said. Her nose

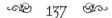

'My name's Lucy,' she said. 'Lucy Partleby.'

crinkled as the last piece of gauze came away. 'Though I don't know about this,' she said, poking at the green ointment beneath.

'It's a sphagnum-moss poultice,' I told her. 'The professor swears by it.'

Lucy laughed. 'Well, I'm not sure what Matron would say, but it certainly seems to be working.' She frowned, her pretty nose wrinkling. 'This is a nasty bite, Mr Grimes. How did you come by it?'

'Please, call me Barnaby,' I replied. 'It's a long story. Are you sure you want to hear it?'

'Quite certain, Mr . . .' Lucy Partleby smiled. 'Barnaby.'

CHAPTER 8

It was dark by the time Will and I left the hospital and, as we stepped out onto the street, the lamplighters had already done their rounds. The tall, cast-iron lights were lit and the main roads were bathed in their golden yellow light.

In High Market Street, Martindale's – a swanky clothes emporium – had recently started a curious trend whereby they placed samples of their produce in the front window of the shop, which they then kept permanently lit. Others had followed suit. Kruger and Syme's, J.F. Tavistock's, Elspeth de la Tour's; all now glowed with light.

A little further on, the bustling Theatre District was similarly well lit, with hissing gas lamps brightening up the ornate frontages of the buildings. Passing by the magnificent Petronelli Playhouse and music halls like the Alhambra and Molly Molloy's, I paused to take in the advertising placards and posters – and wondered whether Lucy Partleby might like to take in a show with me . . .

Will had some night drops to do for the apothecary, so I bade him goodnight and we parted on the corner of Laystall Street and Hog Hill. For myself, I planned to get an early night and, since my arm felt so much better, to try my hand at some simple highstacking at dawn the next day.

I was wandering down the considerably less well-lit streets of my neighbourhood towards my rooms in Caged Lark Lane, when I heard the cheery babble of voices coming from the Goose and Gullet, and suddenly felt ravenously hungry. As I stepped through the door of the tavern, the warm cheerful atmosphere wrapped itself around me like a comforting blanket, and I smelled the delicious aroma of fresh mutton pie.

It was still early in the evening, and the dimly-lit room was barely half full. There were a few tradesmen, young and old, who had stopped by after work, and a trio of flower-women who met up regularly to put the world to rights. Some sat chatting at small round tables in twos and threes, some were standing, while a couple of solitary drinkers propped up the bar.

A short wispy-haired man – a flat Salisbury cap on his head and sleeves rolled up – was playing the battered piano softly in the corner. Head cocked to one side, he was knocking out a familiar music-hall tune, but with soft and delicate flourishes played over the melody, as though he was entertaining himself rather than the other regulars. A black and white dog lay at his feet, fast asleep.

'Evening, Barnaby,' said the landlady, a red-cheeked roly-poly woman who had been head parlourmaid to a duke in her younger days. She was wearing a gaudy red blouse with a high-collar and a spotted apron, and was vigorously polishing a glass with a cloth. 'Haven't seen you here in a while.'

'I've been busy, Betsy,' I said. 'But I've missed your excellent mutton pies . . .'

'Coming right up,' she said, 'with extra gravy, just how you like it!'

'You'll need something to wash it down with, young Grimes,' came a familiar gruff voice to my right.

I turned, to see Blindside Bailey, the news-paper-seller, seated on a high stool at the end of the bar. He turned and fixed me with his one good eye.

I smiled. 'A glass of old cider,' I told Betsy, 'and a pint of ale for Blindside, here.'

'That's very good of you, young Grimes,' he

said. 'Please accept the grateful thanks of an old soldier.' He shifted round on the stool. 'I see you've been in the wars yourself, lad.'

He pointed to my bandaged arm. I smiled.

'Oh, it's nothing,' I said. 'Just a scratch . . .'

'Aye, that it is,' said Blindside. 'That it is, young Grimes, to be sure. But I've seen scratches turn nasty back there in the East. Fester and poison until a leg or an arm is lost . . .' He rapped a dirty finger against his wooden leg. 'And I've seen plenty more besides, lying in a stinking bed in a hell-hole that they called a regimental hospital in the Malabar Kush, trying to recover . . .'

Betsy placed the tankard of ale in front of Blindside. He swigged it enthusiastically, then wiped his mouth on the back of his hand.

'Oh, the tales I could tell, young Grimes,' he said, staring into his half empty tankard. 'The tales I could tell . . .' He lifted the tankard to his lips and drained it in one gulp. 'I don't suppose I've told you the tale of how I lost a fortune in jewels picking up a glass of water?'

'I don't think you have,' I said, as Betsy placed a glass of old cider and a slice of mutton pie in front of me. 'But I'd love to hear it.'

Blindside stared into the bottom of his empty tankard.

'Another ale for Blindside,' I told Betsy, picking up my supper and crossing the tavern to the table by the fire.

Blindside Bailey followed me; ale in one hand, crutch in the other. We sat down opposite each other, the orange-yellow light of the burning coals flickering across his war-ravaged face. He raised his tankard to me, before taking another swig.

'Well, it happened like this,' he said, settling himself back in his chair. 'I was in the hospital, having just lost my leg – though how that filthy barracks came to be called a hospital was beyond me. Mind you, most things *were* beyond me, given the state I was in, drifting in and out of sleep, the fever consuming me and giving me waking nightmares so I hardly knew when I was awake and when I was sleeping . . . Do you know what that's like, young Grimes?'

'I think I do,' I said softly, taking a swig of old cider.

'Anyway, my fever finally broke, and when I became aware of my surroundings once more, I was astonished. The filthy barracks had been cleaned. There was fresh linen on my bed and my poor stump had been dressed in bandages that hadn't even been used before. Why, for a moment there, I thought I'd actually died and gone to heaven. Not surprising really, given that we were tended by angels, dressed in white and carrying lanterns. Ministered to our every need, they did, without complaint or a harsh word. Angels of mercy and no mistake . . .'

Blindside finished off his ale and I ordered him another one. I noticed how the firelight glistened on the tears that had gathered in the corners of his eyes.

'Anyhow,' he went on, 'one night they brought in a forlorn hope and laid him in the next bed from me – the days of sharing four to a bed having been abolished . . .'

'Forlorn hope?' I asked, taking a mouthful of mutton pie.

'That's what we called the hopeless cases, ones that most likely wouldn't live for more than a day or two,' he said. 'But this wasn't just any old forlorn hope, no sir. This was none other than Colour Sergeant Stroyan McMurtagh of the Fighting 33rd – the meanest and most black-hearted scoundrel ever to wear the scarlet coat. He and his three corporals were notorious in the garrison for extortion, brutality and thieving. Back there in the Malabar Kush though, in those dark times, the top brass turned a blind eye to such things, especially when those rogues could fight like lions when called upon to do so. And to be sure they *were* called upon, especially the Fighting

33rd. Always in the thick of it – the fall of Dhaknow, the siege of Rostopov and the storming of the Great Redoubt, the thirty-third regiment of foot led the way. Why, I can still remember Sergeant McMurtagh standing on the ramparts of the Great Redoubt, waving the regimental standard through the gun smoke; the winged Angel of Victory on a sky-blue field . . .'

Blindside Bailey's face had a faraway expression as he gazed into the crackling fire, and I noticed that his tankard remained untouched before him.

'Go on,' I said, intrigued.

'Well, every one of us believed that McMurtagh and his corporals were nigh on invincible, so I was more than a little shocked to see the orderlies carry him in as a forlorn hope. Horribly injured, he was, a gaping hole in his chest and his left arm a jagged stump of splintered bone. The nurses did their best to dress his wounds and sent for the garrison surgeon, a fresh-faced young doctor who had replaced the drunken old sawbones who'd taken my leg. But it was plain that Colour Sergeant McMurtagh wasn't long for this world. He must have sensed it himself for, as he lay there in the flickering lamplight, he seemed to want to unburden himself before he met his Maker. So I sat with him, and did the only thing I could do for him. I listened . . .'

Over by the piano, the dog had woken up and was growling at something only it could see. The man in the Salisbury flat cap stopped playing and leaned down to pat it.

'Turned out,' said Blindside Bailey, pausing to take a swig from his tankard, 'that he and his black-hearted corporals had committed one crime too many. In all those years in the lands of the East, between sieges and rebellions, McMurtagh and his comrades had gone to astonishing lengths to enrich themselves, by robbing palaces, plundering temples and holding petty princes and noblemen for ransom. Of course, they took great pains to cover their tracks and always denied any wrongdoing when challenged – and given their fearsome reputation, that was seldom. But now, as he lay dying, the colour sergeant confessed those misdeeds to old Blindside.

'The four of them, he told me, had amassed a great fortune in jewels and precious objects, which they'd hidden in a certain cave in the dusty hills. But even so, such was their greed, they wanted still more - which is how they came to raid the Temple of Kal-Ramesh, goddess of the notorious Kal-Khee sect . . .'

'I've read about the Kal-Khees,' I interrupted excitedly, 'at Underhill's Library for Scholars of the Arcane. Weren't they a band of assassins for hire?'

'Oh, more than that, young Grimes,' said Blindside, leaning forward in his chair. 'Much more than that. Up in that temple stronghold of theirs, they worshipped the demon goddess Kal-Ramesh, a golden statue with six sword-

Keeper of Souls, Goddess of Death and Gatekeeper to the Underworld . . .

wielding arms, a necklace of jewel-encrusted human skulls and a single eye in the middle of her forehead. Kal-Ramesh, the Keeper of Souls, Goddess of Death and Gatekeeper to the Underworld . . . Of course, to McMurtagh and his gang, it was just one more bit of plunder to add to their haul.

'He told me, as he lay there dying, about how they'd stormed the temple with fixed bayonets and sticks of dynamite, grabbed the statue and fought their way out, while one of their number kept the Kal-Khees pinned down with a mountain cannon they'd borrowed from Thurston's Second Regiment of Horse Artillery. Escaped without a scratch on them, or so they thought . . .'

Blindside paused and, for a moment, I thought his tankard was empty once more, but when I looked, I could see that he'd hardly touched it. The piano-player had started playing a jolly polka that seemed oddly jarring given Blindside's grim tale.

'Corporal Lancing, "Mad Jack" as he was known, was found face down in the regimental latrines, half his head sliced open. Scatter-gun Thompson was the next to go – hanging from a mango tree from a length of rope. Dusty Arnold was found the following day in a narrow alley near the bazaar, a rusting axe embedded in his skull. The garrison was in uproar, the top brass running around like half-plucked fighting cocks, sentries posted at every corner with orders to shoot on sight . . .

'But none of it did any good. McMurtagh told me how they had planned to strip the statue of its jewels, melt it down and add it to their hoard. But when Mad Jack and Scatter-gun had been murdered, Arnold and he had thought better of it. They'd taken the statue from their secret cave hideout and placed it in the bazaar in the dead of night, hoping to placate the Kal-Khees. And it might have worked, but for one thing . . .'

'What was that?' I asked.

'The eye of the goddess, a dark jewel said to be a portal from this world into the next, was missing. In their panic, McMurtagh said that neither he nor Corporal Arnold noticed, but the Kal-Khees did. The statue disappeared from the bazaar that night, and was spirited away back to the temple in the mountains – but not before Arnold received an axe in the head for his trouble. McMurtagh fought his way out of the alley and staggered into the regimental guardroom, before collapsing. A forlorn case if ever there was one.

'As dawn began to break, he cursed the day he'd thought up the plan to rob the Temple of Kal-Ramesh. Then, the colour draining from his face, he spoke of the fortune in jewels and gold which lay hidden in that cave in the mountains.

'"You've listened patiently to my sorry tale, Private Bailey," he whispered, "and I'd like to repay you for your kindness by giving you directions to the hidden treasure trove my crimes have furnished . . ." His voice was cracked and raw as he spoke the words, and I turned to reach for the glass of water by my bed, to offer the dying man a drink. When I turned back, Colour Sergeant McMurtagh of the Fighting 33rd was dead.'

Blindside raised his tankard and drained it to the dregs before placing it dramatically on the table before him.

'Which is the tale, young Grimes, of how I lost a fortune picking up a glass of water,' he said. 'And I haven't touched a drop of the stuff ever since!'

CHAPTER 9

Over the next few days I was up to my wing-tipped collar in work, getting up early and returning to my rooms late, as I struggled to catch up on the two days I'd missed. What was more, in the wake of a severe snowstorm, extra business came my way as clients sent urgent requests to the coal-merchants, roof-tilers and furnace-repairers.

Thankfully, my arm felt right as rainwater and I was back up on the rooftops, high-stacking across the city, making drops all over town – everywhere, in fact, except Gatling Quays, where the gangs were at one another's throats over the disappearance of Firejaw O'Rourke's body, and innocent bystanders were getting hurt. Ma Sorley's Fried Eel and Lobster Shop on Pekin Street got wrecked in a near riot. Then a couple of warehouses – one full of brandy; another, resin – were burned out. The Lanyard Inn, a seedy harbour-side public house, was shut down after a small altercation turned into a street brawl, resulting in two dozen arrests by the Harbour Constabulary.

Each day, as I passed Blindside Bailey on the corner, he had another lurid headline to shout. 'Sumpside Boys Fight Harness Riggers Gang in Firejaw War!' 'Thump McConnell takes on Flour Bag Mob!' 'Fresh Grave Robberies Fuel Firejaw War! Read all about it!'

No one, it seemed, was safe. From the carefully manicured gardens of the Westmede Cemetery in well-heeled Mayvale to the Boiler Road Graveyard in Cheapside, the stories were the same. Graves were being breached and corpses going missing. And each time it happened, it opened up the wounds caused by the missing Emperor, and trouble flared anew down at the quays. For my part, I stayed away from Gatling Quays, and most particularly from Adelaide Graveyard, where I'd had my terrifying hallucination, for that was what I was now convinced it must have been.

Meanwhile, the weather continued to be bitterly cold. Slippery ice and numb fingers and toes make for dangerous highstacking, so the following morning I decided to give Will Farmer some useful tips for winter on his way to St Jude's. We set off in freezing fog at six-thirty. Day was just beginning to break.

'If you're going for a Drainpipe Sluice, check whether there's any frost on the joints,' I said, as we reached the end of a split roof and looked down. I pointed. 'If there is, like on that one, it's too cold to use. Your hands

We set off in freezing fog at six-thirty.

could stick to the metal and then tear away the skin. If it's melted, though, it means hot water has been washed down inside and warmed it up. Like over there,' I said, pointing again. 'We'll take that one.'

Will nodded. A little further on, we stopped again. I nodded to the roof opposite.

'Be careful of black ice,' I told him. 'It's all but invisible, but as slippery as a greased eel. On icy mornings like this, before you set out, you want to put some sand or grit in your trouser pocket. Then,' I said, reaching into mine, 'you can chuck some across to where you're going to land for a better grip.'

'Clever,' said Will.

'Thinking ahead,' I said, and patted the bump halfway down the front of my game-keeper's waistcoat. 'Always think ahead.'

Will frowned. 'What's in there, then?' he asked.

'Sphagnum moss,' I told him, and grinned.

'You're not the only one who's got a drop to make at St Jude's.'

I wanted to see the pretty young nurse again, and this time I had a present for her.

We arrived at the hospital ten minutes later. The place was busier than ever, with the cold foggy weather – coupled with the increase in coal-smoke as people struggled to keep themselves warm – resulting in count-less new cases of bronchitis, pleurisy, pneumonia and other assorted ailments. The tall vaulted ceilings echoed with the insistent clamour of rattling coughs and thunderous sneezes.

'I'll catch you later,' I told Will, as he headed off to the pharmacist's, the package of Tilling's Patent Lung Lozenges he'd brought with him clamped beneath one arm.

I took the stairs to the second landing and made my way along the corridor to the small room where Nurse Lucy Partleby had dressed my wound a week earlier. I knocked softly on the frosted glass panel and opened the door without waiting to be called – and immediately wished I hadn't.

'Excuse me,' I blustered, blushing furiously as I quickly pulled the door to.

'Barnaby,' came a voice behind me, and I turned to see Lucy smiling up at me, those beautiful green eyes of hers sparkling mischievously. She cocked her head to one side. 'You're looking a bit pale.'

'I . . . I just . . .'

'I do sympathize,' Lucy laughed. 'Old Ma Scanlan having her boils lanced isn't the prettiest sight in the world,' she said, crinkling her nose. 'Would you like me to check that arm of yours?'

I nodded. 'If you wouldn't mind,' I said. 'And I brought you this,' I added, pulling the sphagnum moss from my pocket.

'Ooh, flowers,' said Lucy. 'You shouldn't have.'

We both looked at the bunch of damp,

bruised greenery hanging limply from my hand, and laughed.

'It's—' I began.

'I know what it is,' she said. 'That moss your professor swears by.' She led me into the adjacent room and sat me down on a low-backed chair. 'Right,' she said brightly, 'if you'd like to roll up your sleeve please, Barnaby . . .'

I did as I was told. Lucy looked at my arm, an eyebrow arched in surprise.

'You're sure it was this arm,' she said.

'My left arm,' I said. 'Of course.'

She shook her head in amazement. 'But this is incredible,' she said. 'It's healed perfectly.'

'Perhaps you should apply a moss poultice to old Ma Scanlan's boils,' I suggested.

She smiled. 'There really wasn't any need for you to come back at all, was there?' she said.

'Oh, there was,' I said earnestly. 'I'm here

on a matter of the greatest importance.'

'You are?' she said.

'Yes,' I said, reaching into the uppermost pocket of my waistcoat and pulling out two black and gold tickets. 'I have two upper-circle seats at the Alhambra Music Hall for tomorrow evening. Florrie Boyd, the Hightown Nightingale, is topping the bill . . .' I added.

Before she could say anything, the door to the surgery flew open and a forbidding-looking matron burst into the room.

'Come quickly, nurse,' she commanded, giving me a withering look as she spotted the music-hall tickets in my hand. 'Your social arrangements will have to wait. We have a crisis in the admittance hall.'

Lucy gave me an apologetic smile and hurried after the matron, who bustled quickly along the corridor, recruiting more nurses as she went. Soon a regiment of white-aproned angels of mercy was marching behind her down the stairwell towards the sounds of raised voices and angry cries rising up from below.

Curious, I followed, only to find the great hall of St Jude's – usually so orderly – in a state of confusion. At a glance it looked as if half the gangs of the Gatling Quays lay sprawled in disordered heaps on the tiled floor or propped up on benches, supported by the other half.

Sumpside Boys in battered straw caps and blood-stained bearskin coats shouted insults across the prone bodies of Fetter Lane Scroggers at the Ratcatchers, who returned the compliment. Injured Spike-Tooth Smilers shook bruised fists at the Tallow Gang, while the Joinery Blades formed a protective circle round their leader, who lay in a pool of blood, clutching his head.

'And I'm telling you, there's going to be all hell to pay if you have,' Thump McConnell was shouting. 'The whole of Gatling Quays'll

be up in arms. You'll be finished.'

Across the hall, the new leader of the Sumpside Boys, Lenny Dempster – a hulking great thug with indigo tattoos and a shaved head – bellowed back at him. 'If I have! For the tenth time, McConnell, it's them grave-robbers what done it, not us. Don't you read the papers?' He squinted at the boss of the Ratcatchers. 'I take it you *can* read.'

Thump McConnell shook a bloodied fist. 'And who are they anyway, these grave-robbers, eh? I notice that cousin of yours is doing very nicely . . .'

'Yeah,' said Flob McManus, head of the Flour Bag Mob, being helped to his feet by several of his cronies. 'Always flashing the readies, is old Louie, but I ain't never seen him do nuffin' to earn it.'

'Are you saying my cousin's a graverobber?' Lenny Dempster demanded, his hand hovering above the knife at his belt. 'Eh? Are you calling him a graverobber?'

'If the cap fits,' came a squeaky voice, from the crowded benches.

It was Mad Maddox Murphy of the Fetter Lane Scroggers, a second-rate leader of a third-rate gang, who would do anything he could to drive a wedge between the big boys. Thump, Flob and Lenny were having none of it.

'Shut it, Murphy!' they chorused.

Suddenly, Thump McConnell lost patience. He brandished his ham-like fist. 'Let's finish this once and for all now!' he roared. 'Ratcatchers versus the Sumpside Boys – or should I say, dirty lowdown graverobbers?'

'Come on, boys,' replied Lenny Dempster, gathering his gang around him. 'Let's put the new Emperor in the ground . . .'

'What is the meaning of this?' The imperious voice of the matron cut through the air like a hot knife through hog-fat. Behind her, the ranks of the nurses surveyed the chaotic scene impassively.

Instantly, the gang members turned in her direction. The matron on the stairs towered above them, the flickering lamp in her hand casting shadows on her heaving bosom and round face.

'Tobias McConnell,' she boomed, 'is that you?'

The leader of the Ratcatchers swallowed and unclenched his fist sheepishly. He looked round. So did everyone else.

'Yes, ma'am,' he admitted.

'I did not sit up half the night, nursing you through the bloody-croup as a baby, so that you could run amok in my hospital,' she said, her unblinking eyes boring into his.

'And you. Leonard Dempster. Two broken legs, wasn't it?' Her eyebrows knitted together. 'What would your poor dear mother say?'

'Dunno, ma'am,' Lenny muttered. 'Sorry, ma'am.'

'Phoebus McManus! Maddox Murphy. Lawrence Patterson . . .' One by one, she shamed them all. 'That I should live to see the day when you come back to St Jude's, a place of healing, and display such disgraceful behaviour!'

As cowed as whipped puppies, the gang members stared at their boots, their shoulders sloped and heads hanging. The matron crossed her arms.

'My nurses shall dress your wounds and admit the more serious cases to our wards. The rest of you may leave . . . Now.'

The nurses, including Lucy Partleby, sprang into action, efficiently assessing the injuries and treating them as the matron looked on. Meanwhile Thump, Lenny and the other uninjured gang members sloped out of the hospital, muttering under their breath. This clearly wasn't the end of the matter.

Looking down, I saw that I was still clutching the two tickets, and I scanned the hall in search of Lucy, who had yet to answer my question. What I saw banished all thoughts of a romantic evening at the music hall from my mind.

Striding across the hall was a young doctor, a wooden stethoscope in his hand. He wore a long black cape trimmed with ocelot fur and a swanky high hat with a dark-red band. As I watched him make his way through the crowd, Ada Gussage's words from that nightmarish night came back to me.

'He's one of them graverobbers, I'd bet my last brass farthing on it . . .'

CHAPTER 10

The doctor strode towards the door, the metal tips to his boot heels clicking on the polished marble. I followed at a safe distance behind. As I emerged through the doorway, I looked down and saw him at the foot of the steps, climbing into an elegant two-wheeler that a hospital orderly had brought round from the carriage park.

It was being pulled by a fine grey, and my gaze was drawn to the wealth of highly polished brasses which had been attached at the horse's forehead, behind the ears and at the shoulders, with half a dozen more hanging from its martingale. Usually, these days, horse brasses were mere decoration, but I knew that there were still those who believed the amulets could distract the 'evil eye'.

Pools of fuzzy light, thrown out by the two magnificent brass lamps which were fixed to the front of the carriage, spilled out over the pavement. The doctor tipped the orderly with a silver coin and climbed into the carriage. Taking the reins, he gave them a light twitch. The horse whinnied – two long plumes of mist pouring from its nostrils – and, with a lurch, trotted off briskly along the narrow road, the clopping of its hooves and clatter of the carriage wheels echoing back and forth between the buildings on either side.

I gave chase, running down the steps of St Jude's and off along the pavement until I spotted a conveniently positioned drainpipe that offered me a simple and unbroken climb to the rooftops. Thankfully, a thickening fog had slowed the traffic down and as I pulled myself up onto the corrugated iron roof, the carriage was just reaching the junction at end of the street. The two great lamps shone through the fog like saints' halos as the carriage swung round to the left. I picked my way along a long brick parapet wall, then cut back at an angle over the top of a pitched roof, finding myself directly above the cab when it arrived at the next junction.

All round me, the icy fog swirled, as yellow and sulphurous as a witch's brew. It softened the edge to every building, blurring the roof-tops and blotting out the chimney stacks. It smudged the lamplights and muffled every sound. It numbed my fingers, stung my eyes and left a rank metallic taste on my tongue. With the temperature still below freezing point, I needed to heed the advice I'd given Will earlier as I highstacked after the carriage, one eye on the treacherous ledges and drops, the other on those two fuzzy lamplights far, far below me.

At the junction of Gradely Street and Whitlow

Lane, I came to a jump that would normally have given me no problems, but that I simply didn't dare attempt given the treacherous conditions. I quickly assessed the alternatives. There was a stepped gable to my left, but that would have taken me away from the road; there was a square chimney stack to my right, but I could see that the staple-like steps sunk into the mortar were treacherously rusty. Ignoring both, I lowered myself onto a narrow ledge and, with my back and palms pressed against the wall, edged myself along it until I came to the framework of scaffolding I'd spotted.

Manoeuvres involving scaffolding are called Hangman's moves – there's a Hangman's Climb, a Hangman's Descent, a Hangman's Swing and a Hangman's Grapple. Sometimes – when rotten beams of wood were used or when the scaffolders failed to knot the ropes properly – the sinister names of the moves lived up to their reputation. Pat Johnston, a tick-tock lad from the other side of town, had been killed the previous month when he tumbled from badly erected scaffolding.

I eased myself gingerly down onto the upper boards, taking care not to skid on the frosty wood. From there, it was a simple matter to swing one of the planks round till it rested on the roof opposite. I balanced my way along it, arriving safely at the other side and congratulating myself on having invented a new manoeuvre.

I called it a Hangman's Bridge.

A quick glance down confirmed that, below me, the carriage lights were still in view, bearing left onto a broader street. I followed them, keeping pace across the rooftops as the carriage and its mysterious occupant travelled through the fog-bound city, until at last I found myself atop the familiar ridged roof of Sunil's tea warehouse and realized that we were on the Belvedere Mile.

A moment later, my heart sunk. We'd come to Gatling Quays!

To my right was the front of Adelaide Mansions, the light from Ada Gussage's window hazy in the thick mist. The carriage pulled up in front of the building, and I saw the doctor jump down, wrap his cape around him and tether his fine carriage horse to a lamppost. I wondered whether Ada was watching him as well.

Under the cover of the swirling yellow fog that wound itself round me like a mortician's shroud, I descended the building and followed the doctor. He crossed the road and went through the cast-iron archway into the grave-yard. I hesitated, my heart thumping fit to burst in my chest.

Could I summon up the courage to enter that fearful place a third time? I asked myself. Was this doctor meeting his accomplices? I wondered, or simply returning to the scene of his ghoulish crime?

There was only one way to find out for sure. Swallowing hard, I forced myself to enter Adelaide Graveyard once more.

Darting along from yew tree to yew tree, I kept myself hidden both from the doctor and from anyone who might be passing. From somewhere close by, I heard the bells of St Angela's toll. It was midday – though as far as visibility went, it might as well have been midnight. At the far side of the graveyard, I thought I was going to get spotted as the doctor abruptly doubled back – but instead of returning the way he'd come, he squeezed through a gap in the fence where one of the upright rails was missing, then stumbled down the steep slope on the other side.

I held back a minute, waiting for the sounds of slipping and sliding to subside, before going after him. At the bottom of the slope, I looked round me, trying to see which way he'd gone. His footsteps trailed across the wet mud, then disappeared in the direction of the great sewer mouth of Gatling Sump.

Head down, I crossed the upper shoreline.

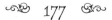

The tide was out and I could see the shadowy figures of mudlarks scratting out on the flats. Scuffle-hunters and long-apron men were roaming the quaysides, taking advantage of the fog to search for any unattended goods; and in the distance I saw the flashing light of a wrecker trying to lure a passing barge onto the mudflats. Ahead of me, the doctor's bowed body was next to the sewer tunnel, his head and shoulders swathed in shadow. I crouched down behind an upturned crate.

The doctor was inspecting what at first glance seemed to be a fallen tree trunk that the ebb and flow of the tide had buried, then revealed in the mud. But as I peered through the gloom, I saw that it was in fact some sort of primitive boat or canoe, fashioned from a single tree. The doctor studied it carefully, from blunt stern to rough-hewn bow which, on its underside, bore tell-tale impressions, seemingly seared into the grain of the wood.

I have to confess that bile rose in my throat at the sight of what I knew to be the bite marks of none other than the black-scaled lamprey - that fearsome sea serpent I had battled in the harbour. At last, the doctor seemed to be satisfied. He rose from his crouching position and returned along the mudflats.

Anticipating his movements, I darted up the bank and vaulted over the railings. I hurried back through the graveyard, hardly daring to look at the gravestones on every side. One thing was for certain, I told myself as I reached the gates, just visible in the freezing fog: there'd be no more highstack carriage-chasing for me. When the mysterious doctor got back to his fine two-wheeler and twitched the reins, there'd be an extra passenger coming along for the ride.

Reaching the carriage, I ducked down and employed a neat trick I'd picked up from the street urchins of Hightown. 'Cobble-grazing' it's called, and involves grasping the wheel

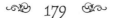

springs beneath the chosen vehicle, and hanging on for dear life. In some of the potholed streets in the rougher districts, it's a recipe for disaster, but on the smooth thoroughfare of Hightown and Carriage Way, it can be exhilarating, believe me.

Grasping the curved springs behind the wheel axle, I wedged my toes into the iron brace of the carriage frame and made myself comfortable. A few moments later I felt the carriage buck and sway as its occupant climbed inside.

The carriage leaped forward, skidded round the corner at the end of Adelaide Mansions and hurtled on down the Belvedere Mile. I glanced down at the bumpy dark-grey road surface speeding past in a blur beneath me. I held on as tight as a barnacle on a barge-hull and tried to determine which way we were going. We turned left, then left again, then right . . . and before I knew it, I'd completely lost my bearings. Once, I fancied I caught the

I wedged my toes into the iron brace of the carriage frame.

whiff of chestnuts roasting on a brazier, which suggested we might be passing through the Theatre District. A while later, I thought I heard the great Bowman bell toll the hour. If I was right, we were heading due north.

A few miles and a lot of arm-jarring potholes later, the carriage clattered over an iron grid and onto the flags of a paved courtyard. Behind me, I heard the creaking of heavy gates rattling shut and the jangling of keys being turned in several locks. The doctor climbed out of the carriage and I saw his muddied boots striding across the courtyard towards a black front door.

Carefully, I unjammed my feet and dropped to the ground. The sound of heavy bolts being drawn back greeted the doctor's knock on the door of what I saw, as I peered from between the spokes of the carriage wheel, was a magnificent town house, screened from the street by a high-walled courtyard of impressive size, and dominated by a large fountain.

As I watched, the door swung open and out sprang a pair of enormous watchdogs, Tannhauser blues, by the look of them. In two great bounds they were beneath the carriage, their slavering jaws inches from my face as I parried them away with my swordstick.

'Walther! Wolfram! Heel!' came a barked command, before an arm reached beneath the carriage, seized me by the collar and dragged me clear.

Looking up, I found myself staring down the barrel of a large-bore hunting rifle.

'I think you've got some explaining to do,' said the doctor coolly.

CHAPTER 11

I rose slowly to my feet, clipping my swordstick to the tail of my waistcoat and raising my hands above my head. The doctor, flanked by the two fearsome Tannhausers, marched me across the courtyard and into the house at the barrel of a gun. Leaving the dogs to roam the courtyard, he closed the heavy front door and proceeded to draw deadbolts across it, top, middle and bottom.

'You're a tick-tock lad by the look of you,' the doctor said, his hunting rifle still cocked and his finger on the trigger. 'How did you come to be skulking beneath the wheels of my Chesney?'

'I was just cobble-grazing, sir,' I began innocently. 'I didn't mean no harm by it, sir, honest.'

'Don't give me that,' said the doctor levelly. 'You're no Hightown urchin. You were following me. Who are you? Are you mixed up in this graverobbing epidemic? Answer me, boy!'

'No, sir,' I protested hotly, despite the menace in his eyes and the rifle pointed at my chest. 'I followed you because a friend of mine told me she'd seen you hanging around the Adelaide Graveyard. I thought *you* might be a graverobber . . .' I took a breath. 'My name is Barnaby Grimes. I *am* a tick-tock lad.' I fished a business card from my waistcoat and handed it to him. 'Professor Pinkerton-Barnes at the university can vouch for me, sir. He'll tell you I'm no graverobber . . .'

The doctor lowered the hunting rifle and, with a sigh, propped it against a mahogany hall table. Taking off his hat and cape, he gave a rueful smile, before handing my card back to me.

'You know, Mr Grimes,' he said, 'I almost hoped that you were part of a graverobbing gang. At least that would be a more plausible explanation than the alternative . . .'

'The alternative?' I said.

'Corpses being raised from the dead,' said the doctor, 'erupting up out of the grave . . .'

'That's what I saw!' I exclaimed. 'In Adelaide Graveyard!'

'You witnessed this?' said the doctor with appalled fascination. His eyes narrowed thoughtfully. 'Come, Mr Grimes, there is someone you must meet.'

The doctor looked genuinely concerned, and there was something about his urgent manner and haunted eyes that made me trust him. He gestured for me to follow him.

We crossed the broad oak-panelled hall, the floor laid out in a herring-bone pattern of polished wooden blocks that creaked as we walked over them. It was cold, and I could see my breath in the grey light which came down at an angle from the small upper windows. Apart from the mahogany table, where the doctor had laid his cape and hat, and a framed water-colour of the outside of the house on the wall beside it, the hall was bare. Our footsteps echoed up the stairwell and round the ceiling.

On the far side of the hall, the doctor stopped in front of the middle of three doors and pulled a key from his pocket. He inserted it into the lock and turned it.

'Go on in, Barnaby Grimes,' the doctor said, as he opened the door and stood to one side to allow me to enter. He gestured towards the plump armchairs and sofas which stood in a cluster around a roaring fire. 'And take a seat.'

Compared with the austerity of the hallway, the drawing room was a treasure trove, luxuriously decorated with items that seemed to have come from the East. There were thick pile carpets in sumptuous reds, orange and aquamarine across the floor, while directly before the crackling fire, lay a tiger-skin rug, the creature's great mouth fixed in a permanent silent roar. Framed silk tapestries depicting jungle scenes hung on the walls, a fluted brass chandelier dangled from a chain at the centre of the ceiling and a hinged four-panelled screen stood beside the mantelpiece which was, itself, crowded with memorabilia; gilt-edged crystal, ivory boxes, silver candlesticks and an ebony incense holder carved in the shape of an elephant, with sweet-smelling smoke coiling from the tasselled howdah on its back.

A large oil painting in an ornate gold frame hung above the mantelpiece. It was a portrait of a handsome woman in a white dress, holding a lamp as she tended a wounded soldier in a night-time hospital ward. As I sat down on a low leather chaise-longue before the roaring fire, and the doctor took his place in one of the two great wingback chairs, I became aware that there was a third figure in the room.

Standing with his back to us, staring out through the bars at the high bay windows, was a stooped aged gentleman with a halo of fine white hair that fell in wisps to his shoulders.

'Father,' said the doctor, in a soft soothing voice. 'It was just as you suspected. I saw it with my own eyes – a primitive canoe beached on the mudflats and uncovered by the low tide, just down from Riverhythe Docks by the Gatling Sump.'

The elderly gentleman gave a low groan.

'And there's more, Father. This is Barnaby Grimes. He's a tick-tock lad who claims to have seen a resurrection . . .'

The old man took a sharp intake of breath. As he raked his fingers through his dishevelled hair I saw that his hands were trembling. Slowly he turned to face me.

'This is my father, Sir Alfred de Vere, Mr Grimes, and I am Dr Lawrence de Vere,' the young doctor said. 'Now, perhaps you'll be so kind as to tell us your story.'

Sir Alfred shuffled over to the second wingback chair and lowered himself into it, his deep-set eyes boring into mine. I shifted round awkwardly in my chair and began. I described my encounter with Thump McConnell – noting how the young doctor's face scowled at the mention of a now-familiar name – and I told them how I and my friend Will Farmer had been invited along to the funeral of the Emperor, gang leader Firejaw O'Rourke. When I got to the part of my tale where, on my chance return to the graveyard, I had seen the Emperor emerge from the grave, both father and son were transfixed.

'Saints alive!' the old man exclaimed. He leaped to his feet, his eyes wild and bony hands a palsy of shaking. 'Then it is true, Lawrence, my worst nightmare has come true!'

'Calm yourself, Father, please,' said the young doctor. 'Think of your heart. Please, take your seat while I fetch your cordial.'

The doctor hurried from the room while his father slumped back in the wingback chair. His face, even in the golden firelight, looked ashen and grey.

'I have meddled with matters beyond human comprehension,' he said. 'Tampered with the very essence of life and death – and now I fear I must pay the consequences . . .'

He fell still. I became conscious of the hissing, crackling sound of the coal burning in the grate, and of the ponderous ticking of a clock somewhere behind me. The old man's face grimaced and twitched as memories came back to him.

'Many years ago, as a young man, I served as a regimental surgeon out East in the

Malabar Kush. The de Veres were a noble family, but had fallen on hard times, and it was all my father could manage to buy – a mediocre commission in an unfashionable regiment. But I didn't mind. I was young, impetuous and full of the arrogance of youth . . .'

As he spoke, his voice grew fainter, and I found myself leaning further and further forward on the chaise-longue to hear the words clearly.

'The Fighting 33rd, they called us, though a worse collection of black-hearted rogues and villains you'd be pushed to find this side of the North-West Frontier.'

My heart missed a beat. The Fighting 33rd? It was the very regiment that Blindside Bailey had told me about . . .

'The officers were no better,' Sir Alfred was saying. 'Too busy living the high life to bother about the men under their charge. The garrison was a disgrace and the hospital barracks even worse. But then Sienna arrived with her angels of mercy . . .'

The old man gazed up at the portrait above the mantel, and his eyes misted with tears.

'Together, we transformed the hospital, saved hundreds of lives and . . . fell in love.' He sighed, and the faraway look in his eyes became troubled. 'And then,' he said, 'I listened to an old soldier's tale . . .'

Outside, a wind had got up. I could hear it whistling through the trees and stirring the dried leaves that still lay upon the ground. It filled the chimney, howling softly and sending soot pattering down into the flames below. As Sir Alfred continued, I felt the hairs on the back of my neck stand on end and, despite the fire, an icy shiver ran the length of my spine.

'This private had been present at the death of the worst black-hearted scoundrel in the Fighting 33rd, whose dark deeds had stirred up a rebellion in the mountains and led to six regiments being despatched to wipe out the infamous Kal-Khee sect of assassins and destroy their temple. Colour Sergeant McMurtagh confessed that he and the three corporals of the colour party had stashed away a fortune in a cave in the hills, but died before he could reveal its location, taking the secret to the grave . . .'

Sir Alfred paused for a moment as he remembered Blindside Bailey's tale – the very same one he'd told me so many years later in the Goose and Gullet. Bailey's had ended with a glass of water, but Sir Alfred's clearly went on.

'A fortune, Mr Grimes. A fortune,' the old man rasped, 'going to waste out there in the bleak wilderness, when one such as I could put it to so much good use. I knew I had to do something, but what?'

He waved a gnarled hand at the artefacts that furnished the drawing room.

'I've always been something of a collector,'

Sir Alfred continued, 'even in those distant days, which is how I came by the last surviving sword of the demon goddess, Kal-Ramesh. In revenge for the murders of the colour sergeant and his three corporals, the high command finally acted. They sent the entire regiment to storm the temple stronghold of the Kal-Khees, which they duly did. The golden statue was hit by a cannon shell and blasted to bits. A bombardier picked up the only remaining fragment, a hand clutching a golden sword, and sold it to me for three shillings. Three shillings! It was the greatest investment I'd ever make.

'You see, Mr Grimes, according to the Kal-Khee assassins, the six swords of the demon goddess each had an extraordinary property. Speed, stealth, strength, disguise, prophecy and . . . life.'

'Life?' I prompted.

'Life. The sixth sword – the one I was lucky enough to have purchased from that unsuspecting soldier – brought sect members back to life. Or so the stories went. Unbelievable, I know, Mr Grimes. And yet you and I both know such things are indeed possible, do we not?'

I swallowed hard.

'At the dead of night, I took the sword to the military cemetery outside the small dusty garrison town where we were stationed and stood before the simple headstones of the murdered colour sergeant and his corporals and planted it in the dusty earth of first one, then the next, and the next, and the next, and . . . nothing happened. At first. Then, as I clutched that demon sword with the golden hand severed at the wrist, I heard it. Scraping and scrabbling. Soft at first, then louder and louder, until . . . first one, then another and another of the colour party *burst* from the ground.'

I shuddered as the memory of Firejaw O'Rourke flooded my thoughts.

First one, then another of the colour party burst from the ground.

'It was then that I realized, to my horror, that not only had it been four weeks since their hasty burial, but that the causes of their deaths – the axe, the rope, the stake – had not been removed. Now there was no point. Putting aside my revulsion, I instructed them to climb to their feet. They did as they were told, their obedience sending a shiver of excitement down my spine.

'"Take me to your treasure," I told them.

'Without a word being spoken, they fell into a line, their feet dragging as they lurched forward. With my lantern in my hand, I hurried after them. We walked for more than an hour through the rocky barren landscape of the Malabar Kush, leaving the sleeping garrison behind, the half-moon shining eerily down as we arrived at last at the side of a wedge-shaped hill. Without pausing, they walked halfway up the steep side of the hill, before stopping on a narrow ledge.

'There, in silence, the four of them fell into

the roles they must have had when still alive. Thompson cleared away a covering of dead scrub; Lancing and Arnold stepped forward to shift a huge slab of rock, to reveal a narrow entrance to a cave. Colour Sergeant McMurtagh entered first. I followed close behind, holding the lantern up to illuminate the inside of the cave.

'It was a dry, dusty place. The walls were pitted and the floors covered in a soft, reddish sand. A regimental flagpole was propped up at the back of the cave. Beside it, in the shadows, lay four enormous chests. Colour Sergeant McMurtagh crouched down and reached into the dark, shadowy recess. A moment later, to the sound of grinding and scratching, he dragged one of the wooden chests, banded with rusting iron, into the middle of the floor.

'In my excitement, I pulled the sword of Kal-Ramesh from my belt and prized open the lid of the chest. As I gazed as its magnificent contents, I dropped the sword in astonishment and fell to my knees, gasping for breath. Even in the semi-gloom, I could see that the chest was full of treasure beyond my wildest imaginings – there were diamonds, rubies and emeralds sparkling in the half-light, together with more gold than I had ever dreamed of seeing in my lifetime . . .

'"Take it outside," I commanded.

'Without hesitation, McMurtagh hefted the chest up onto a shoulder and, lurching from side to side, carried it out of the cave. I followed close behind.

'"Fetch the others!" I told the undead soldiers.

'The colour party stumbled back into the cave and I was about to follow them when there was a strange rumbling sound and the earth beneath me began to shake. I had instinctively seized the treasure chest, and clutching it in a fierce embrace, fell to the ground. Great cracks opened up in the earth as the very hills themselves seemed to shake and shudder with revulsion at what I had done. All I could do was hold on tight and pray that I would survive as rocks slipped, boulders rolled and the air filled with choking clouds of sand . . .'

The old doctor shook his head wearily.

'As earthquakes go, it wasn't, by all accounts, a large one. But on that strange unearthly night, I felt as if hell itself was preparing to swallow me up for my wicked deed. When it stopped and the air had finally cleared, I saw that the entrance to the cave had been sealed up by a massive rock fall. The four undead soldiers of the Fighting 33rd were trapped inside, along with, I only realized later, the sixth sword. But I had no thoughts of that. They could stay there for a thousand years so far as I was concerned. I was alive and rich beyond my wildest dreams!

'I resigned my commission, married my

dear Sienna and returned to this great city of ours and my ancestral seat, where I was able to restore the de Vere family fortunes. And that's not all I did,' Sir Alfred said proudly. 'Together with Lady Sienna, I used my wealth to transform St Jude's Hospital into the model institution it is today. A legacy I shall, one day, pass on to my son . . .'

'But that is not quite the end of the story, is it, Father?'

I looked up to see the young doctor standing in the doorway, his face as ashen and grey as the old man's.

'What one earthquake can bury, another can open up,' he said. 'No wonder those reports of seismic seizures in the East last autumn filled you with such dread. Then the sightings down by the docks near the Gatling Sump – and the sudden wave of grave robberies. With each one, you added another lock, another bolt, another chain to the door, until you yourself are as entombed, here in this great house of yours, as completely as those accursed souls were for all those years . . .'

'Stop it! Stop it!' the old man cried, tearing at his white hair. 'I can't bear to think of it!'

Having seen Firejaw O'Rourke, I knew exactly how he felt.

'The colour party have returned from the East and are here in the city,' the young doctor said. 'I know that now. And they have raised an army against us . . . A legion of the dead!'

'Against *us*?' whispered the old man. 'Oh, no, it's *me* they want. They have come back for revenge!'

Just then, from outside in the courtyard, came the long anguished howl of a pedigree Tannhauser blue.

CHAPTER 12

*T*ogether with Sir Alfred, I leaped to my feet and dashed across the room to the bay windows. It was as black as a collier's coal cellar outside. Starless. Moonless. In the light spilling from the drawing-room, I could see that as night had fallen so the fog had thickened once more, and was coiling and swirling around the courtyard.

Then, as we looked out, the flagstone just beside the fountain slowly rose, like a trap door in a hayloft. The howls of the Tannhausers grew louder, as did the sound of their claws desperately scratching at the front door.

'They're coming for me,' I heard Sir Alfred whisper.

A hideous face – like a ghastly Jack-in-a-box – appeared from beneath the flagstone, its lipless skull-like head grinning insanely. Slowly, it hauled itself out of the sewer tunnel that lay below, and was replaced by another apparition, one-eyed and gaptoothed, its hair a wild crow's nest of black and grey. Then another. And another . . .

I staggered back as the first of them raised a skeletal fist and began pounding at the window. The others followed suit and the blows echoed round the room, louder and louder, until the pane of glass abruptly shattered, sending vicious shards of glinting glass flying inside. A rush of cold air poured into the room, along with the stench of sewers and a pestilential odour of rotting and decay.

With a rattling grunt, the first hideous corpse seized the bars at the window with its bony hands and began shaking them violently.

Others did the same as more arrived, until every bar was encircled by the cadaverous fingers of the corpses as they rattled them in a ghoulish frenzy.

Suddenly, there was a bright flash and an ear-splitting *bang!* sounded in my ear. In front of me, the head of one of the lurching corpses exploded in a mess of teeth, bone and brains. A second shot ran out, and the ribs of a skeleton next to it shattered like the innards of a piano. I spun round to see the young doctor, his eyes wild, standing in the middle of the room with the smoking hunting rifle in his hand, busy reloading. The choking smell of gunpowder hung in the air.

From behind me, there came a *crack* and the splintering of wood. Turning, I saw the entire framework of iron bars coming away from the wooden window-frame, with the headless corpse and shattered skeleton working along with the rest, as the legion of the dead gave an almighty shove and sent the window bars clattering to the floor. The creatures poured over the window-ledge and, crunching glass underfoot, flooded into the room.

The doctor fired again. Once, twice; the bullets smashing into the face of one and the shoulder of another.

'Quick!' he gasped, seizing his father, who was standing frozen to the spot, his mouth open and tears pouring down his face. He dragged him towards the door. 'Mr Grimes . . .'

The three of us stumbled through the doorway. The doctor spun round, locked the door behind him, then slipped the bolt across.

'This way,' he told me.

We ran across the wooden hallway to the corridor opposite. Behind us, the noise of heavy blows and splintering wood resounded as the legion threw themselves at the door. I glanced round to see the glinting of metal as an axe-head was driven through the oak panel. The doctor unlocked a door at the end of the corridor and opened it, to reveal a large kitchen on the other side. We hurried inside, to be confronted by a shadowy figure crouched over a large pine table by the kitchen range. Behind it was a broken window and, as it raised its head, I was confronted with my worst nightmare.

'Firejaw O'Rourke,' I breathed.

He raised his unburned hand and, filthy fingers outstretched, stumbled towards us. Suddenly, I realized that Firejaw wasn't alone. From the shadows all round the great kitchen others emerged – a regiment of graveyard ghouls. One was bloated, her skin blue and grey; another, an emaciated dowager. A knock-kneed boy advanced in step with the skeletal one-armed sailor in a blood-stained uniform to his right . . .

'Back to hell with all of you!' Doctor de Vere shouted at Firejaw. He raised the rifle to his eye and pulled the trigger.

A soft *click* sounded, followed by another.

'Accursed thing,' he spat and, taking the barrel of the rifle in both hands, lunged forward at the advancing corpse. The shaft cracked heavily into Firejaw's head, sending blood and dust and splinters of bone flying across the room. 'Get my father out of here,' he shouted back. 'Quickly, Mr Grimes. I'll hold them off as long as I can.'

I hesitated, uneasy about leaving him.

'Now!'

'This way, sir,' I said to Sir Alfred, taking him by the elbow and steering him through the door and back along the corridor.

From behind us, the sounds of smashing glass and crockery came from the kitchen; ahead, the frenzied battering of the drawing-room door was louder than ever. Back in the hall, the front door abruptly shattered and fell in splinters to the floor. A horde of lurching corpses streamed in, joined from behind us by more, advancing along the corridor from the kitchen.

'Is there a back way out?' I hissed. 'It's our only chance.'

Shaking violently, the old man grabbed my arm and hurried through a door to our left. We passed through a windowless butler's pantry and a box room lined with shelves of crockery and silverware, before arriving at a low battered-looking door with a rusting latch. Without saying a word, Sir Alfred threw himself at it. He pulled the bolts across, top and bottom, turned the key in the lock and lifted the latch.

'I'd better go first,' I said, unhooking my swordstick and stepping forward.

I opened the door and peered out across the broad croquet lawn on the other side, which was bordered by a high wall. The coast looked clear. I turned and nodded to Sir Alfred. We stepped outside, and I wedged the door shut with a garden rake. From inside, came the muffled sounds of destruction as the legion of the dead ransacked the house.

'What have I done?' Sir Alfred murmured miserably. 'Dear sweet Sienna, what have I done?'

All at once, before I could stop him, the old man took off across the croquet lawn towards the high wall opposite. Stopping at a small ivy-fringed gate, he fumbled with his keys, before unlocking it – just as I caught up with him.

'I must go to her,' he gasped, disappearing through the gate.

I followed, and found myself in a small walled graveyard. Glancing at the grand tombs and ornate headstones, it quickly became clear that this was the private resting place of generations of the ancient and venerable de Vere family. Nothing as vulgar as a common public graveyard would do for this aristocratic family, I realized, but instead, a private chapel and a cloistered graveyard where the lords and ladies could rest in peace in their grand tombs.

Sir Alfred was down on his knees in front of a tall white marble sarcophagus, a magnificent winged angel bestriding the arched top. The entire tomb was illuminated by an ornate brass lamp which hung on a chain that dangled from the outstretched right hand of the angel.

'It burns constantly,' Sir Alfred murmured. 'To the memory of my dearest departed Sienna.'

I swallowed nervously. The ghastly apparitions were at the gateway.

There was a wizened hag with a hooked nose and rat's-nest hair. A portly matron, the ague that had seen her off still glistening on her furrowed brow . . . A sly-eyed ragger and a bare-knuckled wrestler, his left eyeball out of its socket and dangling on a glistening thread. A corpulent costermonger; a stooped scrivener, their clothes – one satins and frill, the other threadbare serge – smeared alike with black mud and sewer slime. A maid, a chimney-sweep, a couple of stable-lads; one with the side of his skull stoved in by a single blow from a horse's hoof, the other grey and glittery-eyed from the blood-flecked cough that had ended his life. And a burly river-tough – his fine waistcoat in tatters and his chin tattoo obscured by filth. Glistening at his neck was the deep wound that had taken him from this world to the next.

I shrank back in horror and pressed hard against the cool white marble of the de Vere family vault at my back. Beside me – his body quivering like a slab of jellied ham – Sir Alfred was breathing in stuttering, wheezy gasps. From three sides of the marble tomb in that fog-filled graveyard, the serried ranks of the undead were forming up in a grotesque parody of a parade-ground drill.

'They've found me,' the old doctor croaked, in a voice not much more than a whisper.

I followed his terrified gaze and found myself staring at four ragged figures in military uniform, red jackets with gold braid at the epaulettes and cuffs, who were standing on a flat-topped tomb above the massed ranks. Each of them bore the evidence of fatal injuries.

The terrible gash down the face of one, that had left his cheekbone exposed and a flap of leathery skin dangling. The blood-stained chest and jagged stump – all that remained of his left arm – of the second figure, splinters of yellow bone protruding through the wreaths of grimy bandages. The rusting axe, cleaving the battered bell-top shako, which was embedded in the skull of the third. And the bulging bloodshot eyes of the fourth, the frayed length of rough rope that had strangulated his last breath still hanging round his bruised and red-raw neck – and a flagpole clutched in his gnarled hands.

As I watched, he raised the splintered flagpole high. Gripping my swordstick, I stared at the fluttering curtain of blood-stained cloth, tasselled brocade hanging in filthy matted strands along the four sides. At its centre was the embroidered regimental emblem – the Angel of Victory, her wings spread wide on a sky-blue field, and beneath, the words *33rd Regiment of Foot* written in an angular italic script. The ghastly standard-bearer's tight lips parted to reveal a row of blackened teeth.

'Fighting Thirty-Third!' he cried out, his voice a rasping whisper.

The corpses swayed where they stood, their bony arms reaching forward, with tattered sleeves hanging limply in the foggy air. I smelled the sourness of the sewers about them; that, and the sweet whiff of death. Their sunken eyes bored into mine.

We were surrounded. There was nothing Sir Alfred or I could do. The standard-bearer's voice echoed hoarsely round the graveyard.

'*Advance!*'

From all three sides, the legion of the dead closed in on us. I flicked the catch on my swordstick and drew the blade.

'That won't save us now!' wailed Sir Alfred. 'Nothing can save us . . .'

The words caught in his throat and turned to a strangulated gargle as the tall figure of Colour Sergeant McMurtagh strode towards us. He was clutching a golden sword, gripped by a golden hand, severed at the wrist. Sir Alfred fell back, spread-eagled on his wife's tomb, the glow from the marble angel's lamp illuminating his terrified features.

The colour sergeant brushed past me and I caught the musty odour of death, dust and sea water. Behind him, the three corporals came to a halt, their dead faces inches from my own. With a supreme effort of will, I turned away. The colour sergeant raised the golden sword above his head as he straddled the prone figure of Sir Alfred, who stared up at him, a look of absolute horror on his face.

So this was it. The four soldiers that Sir Alfred had brought back from the dead, all those years ago in the far-off hills of the Malabar Kush, had returned. He had used the demonic powers of the goddess Kal-Ramesh to disturb their eternal rest to enrich himself, and now those undead ghouls had come back to take their revenge on him.

Or so it seemed . . .

Suddenly, the colour sergeant brought the golden sword down with a great scything hammer blow. The blade struck the marble, inches to the right of Sir Alfred's head and shattered into pieces, leaving a single shard embedded in the marble.

For a moment, all was still. Then, from inside the tomb, there came the sound of scuffling and scratching, faint at first, but getting louder by the second. Then, with a crack like a musket shot, the marble fractured round the golden shard, and hairline fissures spread out from it like the tendrils of an exotic plant.

As the stone crumbled and the tomb split apart, Sir Alfred groaned and tumbled to the ground, and out of the cloud of dust the unearthly figure of Lady Sienna de Vere, the angel with the lamp, rose from the grave, now no more than a desiccated skeleton in a threadbare gown of yellowish white.

For one last time, the ghastly sword of the goddess had done its infernal work, and raised the dead.

In front of Lady Sienna, the colour party bowed their ghastly heads and sank to their knees. Then she stepped forward, and as she did so, I saw it. In the centre of the tiara she wore, glowing above the eyeless sockets beneath, was a black jewel.

It was the eye of the demon goddess, Kal-Ramesh.

I suddenly realized that it was *this*, and not poor Sir Alfred, that had drawn these soldiers

It was the eye of the Demon Goddess Kal-Ramesh.

here. This jewel, it seemed, and not revenge, was what they had been seeking so desperately.

All at once, a curling tendril of brilliant light flared from the depths of the jewel and shot out across the graveyard, dividing and dividing again into a thousand different branches. Each one pierced a chest of one of the assembled dead, until every corpse seemed shot through with a dazzling thread of energy.

For a moment they shuddered and trembled, teeth and bones rattling in a hideous percussive dance. Then, in an instant, like the shutting off of a current, the brilliant light cut out, and with it, a ghostly sigh rose from the legion of the dead. And, as I watched, the entire multitude crumbled to dust and blew away in a billowing cloud.

Last to go were the colour party, released at last from their deathly captivity. Before me, in the remains of her shattered sarcophagus, Lady Sienna de Vere crumbled into a pile of disconnected bones.

Faced with the dark jewel's display of extraordinary power, I understood its awesome secret. Where the golden sword, now shattered and in pieces, had had the power to raise and enslave the dead, this black jewel had released them and returned them to eternal rest.

Kneeling, I turned Sir Alfred over and brushed marble dust from his face, to be greeted by two sightless eyes staring back at me. The young doctor came dashing across the grass from the house, the shattered rifle butt grasped in his hand. I looked up at him.

'It's all over,' I said.

He knelt down beside his father.

'Yes,' he said, looking round at me, tears in his eyes. 'It's all over.'

The true nature of the mysterious power that was at work that night I can only guess at.

What I did witness though, was the supernatural influence that the statue of the demon goddess, Kal-Ramesh, exerted on all who came in contact with it.

When they escaped from their prison cave, the colour sergeant and his corporals were drawn to seek out the black jewel – the third eye of Kal-Ramesh – embarking on a journey by dug-out canoe that took them from the lamprey-infested waters of the East to the mudflats of Gatling Quays. They carried with them the instrument of their enslavement, the sixth sword of the goddess. As to how long they must have rowed, riding the ocean currents as they were drawn ever onwards by the black jewel, I can only guess at.

Arriving in this great bustling city of ours, they abandoned their primitive canoe on the mudflats and took refuge in the Gatling Sump. With a twisted logic, the colour party did what they did best. Drawn to graves decorated with winged angels, they used the golden sword to recruit an army – a legion of the dead – to serve beneath the banner of the Fighting 33rd, the Angel of Victory on a blue field. Finally, they homed in on the eye of the goddess, mustering their ghastly troops in the city's sewers for an invasion of the de Vere mansion and its private burial grounds.

And found peace.

A peace of sorts also returned to Gatling Quays, especially after I laid the whole incredible tale out before Thump McConnell and his fellow gang leaders. Argumentative and brutal they may be, but the quaysiders are a superstitious lot. And I've got to say their eyes lit up when they heard about that cave somewhere back there in the East, with three caskets of treasure waiting to be found.

Good luck to any who find it, I say. I'd had enough of six-armed goddesses with eyes in their foreheads to last me a lifetime.

Speaking of which, that strange jewel, the last remnant of the statue of Kal-Ramesh, was buried with Lady Sienna de Vere in a new tomb, joined this time by poor Sir Alfred. He'd had no idea what he was dealing with when he had the strange eye-catching jewel from his treasure trove set in a tiara for his beautiful wife. Perhaps she sensed something of its mysterious power for, according to her son, the young doctor, it had been her favourite piece of jewellery.

Dr Lawrence de Vere closed up the mansion and moved away soon after the events of that terrible night. Not that I blame him. In my opinion, some memories, like people, should remain buried. Before he went though, he paid a visit to the Goose and Gullet, where he met an old soldier of my acquaintance, who had fallen on hard times. I don't like to boast, but suffice it to say that Blindside Bailey now has a pension that means he can buy his own tankards of ale.

As for myself, three weeks later, I found myself highstacking over to St Jude's hospital with my good friend and promising high-stacker, Will Farmer.

He had a drop to make.

I was in search of an angel of mercy, two tickets to the upper circle of the Alhambra Music Hall burning a hole in my pocket.

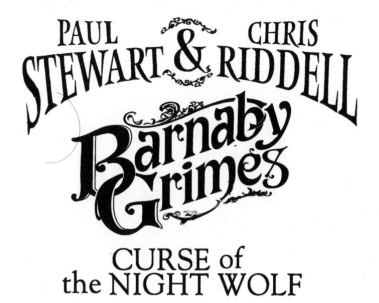

PAUL STEWART & CHRIS RIDDELL

Barnaby Grimes

CURSE of the NIGHT WOLF

One moment I was standing there, sword raised, knees trembling. The next, in a blur of fur and fury, the hellish creature was flying towards me, its huge front paws extended and savage claws aiming straight at my hammering heart . . .

Barnaby Grimes is a tick-tock lad – he'll deliver any message anywhere any time. As fast as possible. Tick-tock - time is money! But strange things are afoot. One moonlit night, as Barnaby highstacks above the city, leaping from roof to roof, gutter to gable, pillar to pediment, a huge beast attacks. He barely escapes with his life. And now his friend Old Benjamin has disappeared . . .

A gloriously macabre tale in a breathtaking new series, packed with intrigue, horror and fantastic illustrations.

PAUL STEWART & CHRIS RIDDELL

Barnaby Grimes

RETURN of the EMERALD SKULL

My grip tightened on the cruel stone knife, the blade glinting, as the blood-red ruby eyes of the grinning skull bore into mine. Inside my head, the voice rose to a piercing scream. 'Cut out his beating heart – and give it to me!'

Barnaby Grimes is a tick-tock lad on a mission - to collect a parcel from the docks and deliver it to a famous school. But dark forces have been released and, as Barnaby returns to Grassington Hall School, he is about to find out the full extent of the horror.

A spine-tingling tale of a school in the grip of a terrible curse. Tick-tock, time is running out. Can Barnaby survive?

THE EDGE CHRONICLES

THE QUINT TRILOGY

*Follow the adventures of Quint
in the first age of flight!*

THE CURSE OF THE GLOAMGLOZER

Quint and Maris, daughter of the most High
Academe, are plunged into a terrifying adventure
which takes them deep into the rock upon which
Sanctaphrax is built. Here they unwittingly invoke
an ancient curse . . .

THE WINTER KNIGHTS

Quint is a new student at the Knights Academy,
struggling to survive the icy cold of a never-ending
winter, and the ancient feuds that threaten
Sanctaphrax.

CLASH OF THE SKY GALLEONS

Quint finds himself caught up in his father's fight
for revenge against the man who killed his family.
They are drawn into a deadly pursuit, a pursuit that
will ultimately lead to the clash of the great
sky galleons.

'The most amazing books ever'
Ellen, **10**

THE EDGE CHRONICLES

THE TWIG TRILOGY

*Follow the adventures of Twig
in the first age of flight!*

BEYOND THE DEEPWOODS

Abandoned at birth in the perilous Deepwoods,
Twig does what he has always been warned not to
do, and strays from the path . . .

STORMCHASER

Twig, a young crew-member on the Stormchaser
sky ship, risks all to collect valuable stormphrax
from the heart of a Great Storm.

MIDNIGHT OVER SANCTAPHRAX

Far out in Open Sky, a ferocious storm is brewing.
In its path is the city of Sanctaphrax . . .

'Absolutely brilliant'
Lin-May, 13

**'Everything about the Edge
Chronicles is amazing'**
Cameron, 13

THE EDGE CHRONICLES

THE ROOK TRILOGY

*Follow the adventures of Rook
in the second age of flight!*

THE LAST OF THE SKY PIRATES

Rook dreams of becoming a librarian knight,
and sets out on a dangerous journey into the
Deepwoods and beyond. When he meets the last sky
pirate, he is thrust into a bold adventure . . .

VOX

Rook becomes involved in the evil scheming of
Vox Verlix – can he stop the Edgeworld falling into
total chaos?

FREEGLADER

Undertown is destroyed, and Rook and his
friends travel, with waifs and cloddertrogs, to a new
home in the Free Glades.

'They're the best!!' *Zaffie*, 15

'Brilliant illustrations and magical storylines'
Tom, 14

COMING SOON

THE IMMORTALS

Five hundred years into the the third age of flight and mighty phraxships steam across the immensity of the Deepwoods, plying their lucrative trade between the three great cities. Nate Quarter, a young lamplighter from the mines of the eastern woods, is propelled on an epic journey of self-discovery that encompasses tournaments, battles, revolutions and a final encounter with the Immortals themselves.

WATCH OUT FOR THE FINAL EDGE CHRONICLES BOOK IN SEPTEMBER 2010!